The Sinner's Gamble

Merry Farmer

THE SINNER'S GAMBLE

Cover design by Dar Albert, Wicked Smart Designs

ASIN: B0B14H1VST

Paperback: 9798833938799

Click here for a complete list of other works by Merry Farmer.

If you'd like to be the first to learn about when the next books in the series come out and more, please sign up for my newsletter here: http://eepurl.com/RQ-KX

❀ Created with Vellum

Chapter One

London – May 1815

"Sir, he's back again."

Caesar sighed and set down the quill he'd been using to reconcile the books for Perdition, the gaming hell he owned and operated with his partners. He scrubbed his hands over his stubbly chin for a moment before staring at the young and eager figure of Stewart, one of the club's—for lack of a better word—footmen in the doorway.

"Can you not just tell him to go away?" Caesar asked, leaning back in his chair. He had other problems to deal with at the moment. Balancing accounts and coming up with new ways to draw in London's finest so that he and his business partners could relieve them of their wealth while entertaining them to the fullest were the least of them.

Stewart continued to stand in the doorway, squirming. "I would, but you know, Mulgrew is...he is a man of the cloth, sir."

"So?" Caesar shrugged one shoulder, his insides

1

buzzing with irritation. And it was irritation, not something else. Certainly not interest or fascination or...or hope. The handsome, irrepressible Rev. George Mulgrew had been a thorn in his side for months now, but it had nothing to do with the fact that he liked to be poked.

Stewart clearly viewed the persistent curate with different eyes. "I...I wouldn't feel right, sir, just going up to a holy man and telling him to bugger off."

Caesar suppressed the warm shudder that passed through him at the image of Mulgrew buggering that came to mind. He sighed, genuinely put out that he was being called away from his work for such a thing, and stood.

"I will see to things myself," he said striding across the room.

He didn't bother to grab his finely-tailored jacket as he pushed past Stewart and out the door. It wasn't as though he was on his way to Almack's, or his father's house, for that matter. The linen shirt and silk waistcoat he wore were good enough for the likes of Rev. Mulgrew.

Despite the onerous task ahead of him, Caesar smiled as he left his office at the back of the ground floor and headed into the heart of the club.

Perdition was his pride and joy, and that of his partners: Jasper Black and Simon Beaumont. They'd purchased the entire building on Jermyn Street, thanks to a discreet transfer of funds from Caesar's father and sources belonging to some of the other partners, and transformed the place from its dull and uninteresting past as a residence into a thriving scene of nightly financial chaos and debauchery.

It continued to look as boring as possible on the outside, but once a man with enough blunt to pass through its doorway entered, he was met with vibrant color, sumptuous furnishings and decorations, and every sort of vice he could possibly wish for. Perdition's card tables were quickly gaining a reputation for excitement throughout London, but there were other gambling pursuits to be had as well, not to mention every sort of company a man of any sort of taste could ask for.

The upper floors were still set up as a residence, though one wing of the house was used by the men and women who provided company for the gamblers. As Caesar passed the grand staircase that led up to his own quarters and those of his partners who resided in the house with him, Jasper was coming down.

"It's early for you to emerge from the office," Jasper said with a smirk as he momentarily fell into step with Caesar. "Do not tell me that our situation is so dire that you've already calculated our demise."

Caesar laughed and shook his head. Jasper knew full well that the Perdition Club was thriving and making them all wealthy men. His suggestion that they were in trouble was a jest only, and a silly one at that.

"I've just been informed Mulgrew is back," he said, sending his partner a flat look.

Jasper swore and lost his merriment. "That's every day this week," he sighed. "Does he think he might actually save souls with his babbling and pleading?"

Caesar's mouth twitched momentarily at the idea of Mulgrew pleading. "I have no idea what the man's intent in pestering us is. He obviously wants something, since he's back again."

Evidently, Caesar had done a poor job of hiding his fascination with the pesky cleric. Jasper smirked at him and said, "I trust you plan to give it to him."

Caesar was a good enough sport to grin and wink at his friend. "That would chase him off for good," he said.

Whether he truly wanted Mulgrew to go away for good was an entirely different matter. Having a curate buzzing around their door like a black fly was bad for business. Even if Caesar and his partners failed to care a whit about their immortal souls or what some unseen god wanted to do with them, the men of substance who patronized the club were made uneasy by the reminder of their own mortality. Enough of them believed the censure of the church—or at least believed their reputations would be damaged if they were discovered to have partaken in half of the activities at Perdition—that Mulgrew's holy admonishments frightened them away.

They'd reached the front hall and paused. It was early in the day, but someone was always patronizing the club, risking their fortunes and their livelihoods at the card tables, or enjoying the company of the beautiful and barely dressed women and men Caesar and his partners employed. Caesar glanced quickly into the closest parlor and spotted a particularly prominent Member of Parliament sitting cozily on a settee in one corner, an angelic-looking young man wearing barely more than a loin cloth on his lap. The lad, Giles, had his hand down the front of the MP's breeches while the man whispered something in Giles's ear that had him blushing.

Caesar's smirk deepened, and he winked at Giles, congratulating him for a job well done. Caesar knew for a fact that the MP in question had just come into a great deal of money by illegally speculating on a matter that had been discussed confidentially in Parliament, and if the man wanted to spend a portion of that on sin and vice in Perdition, then so be it.

It was men like that who Mulgrew and his sermonizing tended to chase away. Sure enough, as Caesar stood close to the club's front door, he could hear the impassioned drone of Mulgrew's voice on the steps outside.

"Sounds like he's made himself a pulpit on our doorstep," Jasper sighed, frowning at the door.

"I'll take care of it," Caesar growled, heading for the door.

London was awash in sunlight and all the colors of May as Caesar opened the door and stepped outside. As dark and sinful as the goings on inside the club were, he and his partners had gone to great lengths to make the façade of the house appear as fresh and beautiful as any of the other homes and clubs in the area. St. James's was a popular spot for gentleman's clubs, not to mention other gaming hells, like Perdition. The area had a patina of wealth and respectability to it, though, which was probably why establishments like his were left alone, for the most part, as long as they kept up appearances. The building itself was kept clean and polished, the gardens around it were regularly tended, and Caesar even paid a few enterprising boys to keep the street in front of the club swept and clear of refuse.

And there, in the midst of all that care and consideration, looking like a broken angel fallen from the heavens, was Rev. George Mulgrew.

"The wages of sin are death," Mulgrew pleaded with the tiny handful of people who had stopped in front of the club to listen to his ranting. "Turn away from this darkness now, while you still can."

Caesar wasn't even certain Mulgrew had heard him come out of the building. He inched to one side and leaned against the doorframe, crossing his arms and grinning at his thorn.

"Gambling is only the beginning of the dark and deadly road this club will set you on," Mulgrew continued. "You will not only lose all of your hard-earned wages, you will lose your morality, your connection to the Almighty. You will lose your very soul."

Caesar tried and failed to hide his grin. It was quaint that Mulgrew believed the street sweepers and working men who had stopped to listen to his piffle were the ones who patronized the club. It was almost sweet that he thought the money being won and lost—usually lost—inside of Perdition's walls came from honest labor and not inheritance or market speculation—which was just another kind of gambling. Caesar wondered what the irritating man would think if he knew where the gold that flowed through Perdition's veins came from...or where much of it ended up.

"It is never too late to repent," Mulgrew went on, still not realizing Caesar was right behind him—which suited Caesar just fine. It gave him a perfect view of the man's outstanding arse and shapely legs, his broad shoulders, and just a hint of skin above the man's collar. He rather thought he'd like to nibble on that skin until Mulgrew sighed his name and begged for more.

Caesar chuckled at himself, wondering how Mulgrew would feel about being the object of his lusts. The poor thing would probably expire in horror at the idea. Which, of course, only made Caesar want the man more.

"It is never too late to turn away from the Devil's path and to return to God's grace," Mulgrew went on. "It is never—"

He must have noticed the way his meager audience was no longer looking at him, but rather, past him. Mulgrew stiffened and turned sharply to Caesar. For a moment, his eyes went wide, and a deep flush painted his cheeks.

6

The man had a beautiful face. His jaw was square and masculine, his lips were full and ripe for kissing, and his eyes were a rich brown and filled with fire. A part of Caesar hoped that fire was for him and not God. It was a sin of its own kind to waste such passion on a creator that Caesar wasn't even certain existed.

"You," Mulgrew said, his moment of shock giving way to a deep frown. "You, more than anyone, should repent and set out on a new path before it is too late."

Caesar pushed away from the doorframe and sauntered closer to Mulgrew, staying one step above him.

"Too late for what?" he shrugged, keeping his posture easy and arrogant.

Mulgrew scowled at him. "Too late for your immortal soul. Too late to enjoy the fruits of Paradise that our Lord guarantees those of us who walk the narrow path."

Caesar shrugged. "Why wait for the fruits of Paradise later when I can enjoy the wine of Perdition now?" he asked, sending a glance to his club.

One of the sweepers who had stopped to listen to Mulgrew chuckled, then went on with his work. Once he left, the others who had lingered to watch moved on as well.

Caesar was surprised when Mulgrew let out a sigh of regret and watched them retreat. The man seemed far more distressed to lose his audience than Caesar thought he should be. That raised all sorts of curious feelings in him. Mulgrew didn't actually *care*, did he? Men like him never really cared, they just liked to hear the sound of their own voices.

"Soon it will be too late," Mulgrew said, fretting. Caesar wouldn't have been surprised if the man had started wringing his hands like an old fishwife. "Soon we will all be damned."

"Damned?" Caesar laughed. He would never understand the dramatics of good people.

Mulgrew narrowed his eyes, likely over being laughed at. "You do not take your salvation seriously enough, sir," he insisted. "The Bible is very clear on the fate of sinners."

"So what if I am a sinner?" Caesar shrugged again. "I am happy, I am amused, and I have my fill of every sort of pleasure whenever I want it."

He couldn't help but sweep Mulgrew's form with a covetous look as he spoke. He had *almost* every pleasure he wanted.

Mulgrew's face went red and his eyes blazed with fire, but it was difficult to tell precisely what sort of fire the man had within him.

"The pleasures of the flesh are hollow indeed," Mulgrew insisted. "It is the eternal pleasures of God's kingdom that we should strive for."

"How do you know?" Caesar said with a grin. "Have you ever enjoyed them?"

"I fully intend to live eternally in the pleasures of God's kingdom when I pass on from this life," Mulgrew said.

"No, I mean the pleasures of the flesh," Caesar said, one eyebrow raised. "Have you ever enjoyed them?"

Mulgrew flushed such a dark shade of red that Caesar's cock twitched in notice. The man was wasting himself on trifling matters of religion, that much was certain.

Mulgrew was saved from answering Caesar's impertinent question as a gentleman Caesar knew to be a freshly-minted viscount approached the club.

"Turn back from your sins," Mulgrew shouted at the man so suddenly that the viscount stumbled backward and nearly toppled over. "Turn away from this den of iniquity. Your eternal life depends on it."

The viscount's jaw dropped, and he stood there, flapping uselessly for a moment, before turning and running.

Caesar was no longer amused by his banter with the handsome curate, not when he cost the club business.

"Enough from you," he snapped, scowling at Mulgrew. "I didn't come out here to play children's games. You have darkened our doorstep long enough. It is costing us business, and I will not have it anymore. Get gone, and stay away."

Instead of cowering and doing as Caesar said, like most men did, Mulgrew seemed encouraged by his telling off.

"My work here has had positive effect, then?" he asked. "Is that what you are saying? I have saved souls by turning potential sinners away from the grandest sinner of all?"

Caesar sighed and rubbed a hand over his face. Mulgrew wasn't just a thorn in his side, he was a canker that would eat through to the heart of his business if he was left alone.

And Caesar most certainly did not want to leave the man alone.

"Very well," he said, making an instant decision, though perhaps a rash one. It was a gamble he had to take, though. For Perdition and for himself. "If you are so certain you know what takes place within these walls, if you are so confident you are saving souls by meddling in business that does not concern you, then come inside and see what you are railing against for yourself."

Once Caesar had Mulgrew inside the club's walls, where no one on the street could see or hear what might befall him, he could deal with the meddlesome man in his own way.

Mulgrew flinched away from him at first, but the unmistakable sparkle of curiosity lit his eyes. "I could not," he said, though Caesar had the feeling those words were meant to be an admonition for himself.

"Certainly, you could," Caesar said with a warm smile. "You would be my guest. You must have been curious about the sort of sin and vice you've been railing against all this time. Wouldn't it confirm everything you've been preaching for God only knows how long now to peek inside the Devil's den and to catch him at his handiwork? You would certainly have much more to shout about."

Madly, that argument seemed to sway Mulgrew. Caesar stepped back and opened the door, then turned to offer Mulgrew his hand. It was like a scene out of an opera, right before the hero sold his soul to the devil and followed him through the gates of hell to his damnation. Caesar intended to make the whole voyage worth Mulgrew's time, though.

Mulgrew cleared his throat, then stepped forward, following Caesar. "Yea, though I walk through the valley of the shadow of death," he recited to himself in a low hum.

Something sizzled in Caesar at the tone of Mulgrew's voice. He wouldn't mind the man whispering filthy things to him in that tone, particularly if the two of them were naked and sweaty. He laughed at that thought, shook his head, and stepped deeper into the front hall, holding the door open for Mulgrew.

Perdition did not disappoint. From the moment Mulgrew stepped inside and Caesar shut the door behind him, the club played its role perfectly. Mulgrew's eyes went wide and his whispered prayers stopped as he glanced around at the dark opulence of the place. He took in the furnishings and the lurid artwork, the gaming tables in the parlor off to the right, and Giles and the MP—who had advanced from mere whispering to Giles sitting astride the man's lap, naked, with his head tilted back as the MP enjoyed him—in the parlor to the left.

Caesar noted with mild surprise that one of the female whores was similarly entertaining a man who he believed was a baron deeper into that same parlor. He also noted the way Mulgrew's gaze lingered on Giles and the MP, not the woman. That small detail made Caesar's blood pump harder and his breeches feel tighter than a vise. Perhaps it was his lucky day if Mulgrew was inclined that way.

"Ah, Caesar, who is your charming friend?" Simon asked as he walked up from the long hall that led to the back, where the office and the stairs leading down to the servants' hall—and a collection of rooms for patrons with more extreme interests—were located.

"Simon, I'd like you to meet Rev. George Mulgrew," Caesar said, grinning at Mulgrew like a cat who had caught the church mouse. "He's just agreed to stop his doorstep sermonizing and to leave Perdition alone."

Mulgrew blinked, still a bit stunned. Then Caesar's words sunk in, and he scowled. "I have agreed to no such thing," he said, inching away from Caesar. "You have lured me into this den of sin under false pretenses. I am here to do the Lord's work, not to wallow in wickedness."

Although, as Caesar noted, his eyes snapped quickly to the particular sort of wickedness Giles and the MP were getting up to, and the blush on Mulgrew's face had slipped tantalizingly down his neck.

"You invited me into your house of damnation to see these evils for myself," Mulgrew went on, "and I have seen them. I could alert the authorities to these evils, these crimes. Surely, none of this is legal." He threw out his arm to Giles and the MP in the parlor.

That was all the signal Caesar needed to know that his

niggling little problem had turned into a far more serious one. Mulgrew was right—a great many activities in Perdition were *not* legal. They'd been protected from the law so far—thanks to the connections that both he and his partners had—but even the most secure protection could not help them evade detection forever, particularly if someone like Mulgrew got it into his head to call them out publicly for it all.

"I was right to rail against this place," Mulgrew said, moving as if he would bolt for the door.

Caesar did his best to keep calm. He couldn't let Mulgrew go now. He hadn't intended to let the man go until he'd changed his mind in the first place, but now his plan had to be more than a lark.

He cleared his throat and gestured for Simon to bring him the bottle and one of the linen handkerchiefs that sat on a small table beside the doorway to one of the parlors as Mulgrew started spouting Bible verses.

"Take no part in the unfruitful works of darkness, but instead expose them," Mulgrew quoted, moving closer to the door.

Caesar rolled his eyes and shifted to block Mulgrew's way as Simon uncorked the bottle and poured a generous amount onto one of the handkerchiefs, holding it at arm's length.

"Calm down, man," Caesar told Mulgrew. "I'm not letting you go out there in this state. You've hardly seen anything, and you've drawn the wrong conclusions from what you have seen."

"I have eyes, sir," Mulgrew fired back indignantly. "I can see what this place is all about."

Simon moved carefully toward Caesar, who extended his arm to take the soaked cloth from him.

"And what is it about?" Caesar asked. "What do you see around you?"

"Vice and...and sodomy," Mulgrew said. "Right before my eyes."

Indeed, Giles was now bouncing on the MP's lap in a particular way.

Caesar shrugged. "There's nothing wrong with a little sodomy. I quite enjoy it myself. I'd wager you would too, if you'd give it a try. I think you'd enjoy it quite a bit."

Mulgrew's eyes went wide. "How dare you suggest such sin to me? I would never—"

That was as far as the gorgeous, pitiable, misinformed man got. Caesar swept Mulgrew into his arms with an iron grip and clapped the soaked handkerchief over his mouth. Within moments, Mulgrew gave up his struggling and groaned as he passed out. It was unfortunate that he had to resort to ether to subdue the man—they kept ether on hand for when patrons of the club became particularly distressed by their financial losses and threatened to turn violent—but Caesar couldn't risk his livelihood, that of his partners, or the lives and reputations of Perdition's patrons by letting Mulgrew run away and reveal what he'd seen.

Quite the contrary. The only way Perdition would be safe to continue on and provide what was necessary for all was if Caesar could convince Mulgrew that he actually craved what he said he despised. And the only way to do that was to give him everything he never knew he wanted and more.

Chapter Two

He'd stepped into Perdition, and he hadn't even lasted a minute before he was doomed.

That thought floated at the top of George's foggy mind as he came out of whatever stupor he'd fallen into. His body felt as though it weighed five times as much as usual, and he couldn't move it for the life of him.

For the gate is wide and the way is easy that leads to destruction, and those who enter by it are many. The verse somehow penetrated the haze in George's mind. Twined along with it, though, was the fleeting thought that Perdition was beautiful. He'd rarely seen such a grand house or so much artwork in one place. His father's house was a dull, lifeless hovel compared to the small glimpse George had had of Perdition from the front hallway.

His thoughts flitted from the pristine marble of the hallway to the fine carpets of the parlors...to the nubile young man who had been enjoying himself in the parlor.

Arousal mingled with the heavy, cloudy thoughts that fought to push themselves to the fore of George's consciousness. He hadn't actually seen what he'd thought he'd seen...

had he? There had been rumors that Perdition hosted more entertainments than just cards, but the young man hadn't been anything like any of the unfortunate, bedraggled women his father had dragged him to preach at around Seven Dials or the Isle of Dogs. He was healthy and well-fed and...and he'd been enthusiastically enjoying his activities.

George's cock stirred again at the memory and he swallowed hard to fight the feeling. Arousal was the very worst of sins, or so his father had always insisted. The man had flogged himself mercilessly whenever the poor harlots he'd dragged George to preach to had excited him, and he'd praised George for not falling prey to their wiles. It was one of the only things he'd praised George for, although if his father had had even the slightest inkling about the things that aroused him, it would have been a different story.

Arousal was the very last thing George wanted to think about in that moment, though. As his mind slowly cleared from the ether he'd been surprised with, his current situation rushed in on him. He'd allowed that devil, Caesar Potts, to lure him into his lair, and now he was a prisoner. He was....

Dear God, he was naked.

George sucked in a breath and snapped his eyes open as the odd sensations he'd felt against his body suddenly made sense to him. He was lying in a bed, arms and legs stretched akimbo, and he was naked. Granted, his body was completely covered, up to his neck, with a blanket, but underneath it, he was unmistakably naked.

He tried to move his arms and legs to sit and reach for the blanket, but he could move no more than an inch. A wave of panic hit him as he realized he'd been tied to the bed. His wrists and ankles were bound with some sort of soft cord, and he'd been pulled spread-eagle. There was very little give in his bonds, so that even when he struggled, he could barely move from his enforced position of repose.

That set George into a panic almost at once. His breathing turned desperate and shallow, and his pulse pounded in alarm as he fought against his restrictive bonds.

"Easy, easy," a deep, soft voice said from beside him. "Don't struggle. You're in no harm."

George wanted to laugh over that ridiculous statement, but his head hadn't completely cleared yet. It pounded, and he was more than a little dizzy as he glanced around, searching for the voice.

He didn't have to search far. The smug, grinning figure of Potts himself stood from where he'd been sitting in some sort of window seat, reading something, and walked to the bed. As casually as you please, Potts moved to sit on the bed near one of George's bare feet, propping his shiny, Hessian boots on the coverlet. Potts leaned back against the tall, thick bedpost and crossed his arms, smiling at George as though he were about to pick him apart and devour him.

George's cock twitched again—more than twitched—which it absolutely should not have done, given the circumstances.

"Wh-here am I?" he asked, cursing his voice for coming out so groggily.

Potts chuckled, crossing his ankles where they rested just inches from the exposed underside of one of George's outstretched arms. "You're in Perdition," he said, as if informing George he was lazing by the Serpentine in Hyde Park.

He was in Hell, of course. That would explain the infernal fire that seemed to burn through him as Potts swept the shape of his covered body with a covetous grin.

George shook his head, clearing his mind a bit more. He hadn't died, he had merely followed Potts inside of his blasted club. But that didn't explain the bed he now lay in, or the calming blue of the wallpaper, the paintings of the seaside that decorated the room...or the expertise of the way the silken cords were tied around his wrists and ankles and, as he could see when he lifted his head a bit, the skill with which they were fastened to the head and footboards of the bed.

"This cannot be the club," he said, still catching his breath after the panic of waking to find himself where and how he was. "You've moved me somewhere. Where am I?"

"I can assure you, good reverend, you are still in Perdition," Potts said, clearly making fun of him. There was too much sparkle in the man's deep, blue eyes, too much color in his strong, stubbly face. His manner was too easy for a man whose soul was in peril.

"This is not a dark and seedy hellhole," George said, nearly sighing, as he lay his head back against the pillow and stared up.

Stared up into a painted canopy of naked and engorged young men enjoying each other in obscene ways and in any number of positions.

George caught his breath, and his cock throbbed even more insistently. He closed his eyes to block out the canopy, but he could not chase away what he'd seen—above him, and sitting at the foot of the bed, gloating over him.

"You're upstairs," Potts explained in an annoyingly pedestrian voice. "This is my bedchamber."

George opened his eyes again and frowned at the man. "You live here? You live in your own hell?"

Potts laughed. "I own the entire building, along with my partners," he said. "Yes, we operate a gaming hell out of the lower floors, and another sort of endeavor upstairs in the other wing. This wing contains our living quarters, though."

It was such an ordinary, simple explanation on the surface, though George caught the whiff of sin in the implication of what the rest of the house was used for.

"Let me go," he said, tugging at his bonds again. "You cannot keep me here, tied to your bed like this."

"Can't I?" Potts said, arching one eyebrow like the villain he was. He uncrossed his arms and reached one hand to the cord binding George's ankle, just inches away from where he sat. He picked up the edge of the blanket and slid his hand under it, caressing George's ankle and calf. "It seems to me that you are in no position to say what I can and cannot do, Rev. Mulgrew."

George sucked in a breath and fought as valiantly as he could not to feel the shivers that shot through him at Potts's touch. He had so little experience with being touched, though. His flesh was sinful, even if his mind fought....

He sighed, giving up the struggle and squeezing his eyes shut. His father's voice was loud in his head, but he was exhausted by it. He was weary to the marrow of his bones, and fighting against something that felt as good as Potts's hand on his calf seemed agonizingly pointless. He couldn't remember the last time he'd slept in a bed as soft and comfortable as the one he was in now. His father insisted that bodily comfort was a gateway to sin, but being cushioned by wool and covered with silk merely made him want to sleep. Even with his body stretched in humiliating bonds.

No, he had to fight it. If he gave up, he was no better than the wretched young man downstairs who had clearly sold his favors to the lecher enjoying him.

With a renewed surge of righteousness, he sucked in a breath and opened his eyes. "How do you know my name?"

he asked. "You introduced me by my name downstairs... earlier." In truth, he had no idea how much time had passed. Enough for Potts to undress him and tie him to his bed.

Dear God, Potts had already seen him naked.

Potts smiled at him, though not unkindly. More like a lion who wanted to play with his prey before devouring it. "You've been menacing us for months now," he said. "Ever since the weather began to warm. You cannot imagine that I would not inquire after the name of the nuisance that has perched himself on my doorstep and frightened away my business for months, can you?"

George frowned. "If I have turned away just one or two souls in peril, then I have done my duty to God and to...." He didn't finish his sentence. He didn't like the answer that immediately came to his mind. He didn't do what he did for his father, he did it because...because it was his divine duty as a man of God. Wasn't it?

"Firstly," Potts said, adjusting the way he sat, though he did not remove his hand from George's calf. If anything, he slid it higher, "you did not turn those men away from this so-called life of sin you seem to think the rest of us who enjoy life are living. You merely sent them to another hell, one that is likely just as bad and not as well looked after."

George scowled and clenched his jaw at that point— mainly because it was probably correct.

"Secondly," Potts went on, "God created us all to enjoy ourselves and His creations. It is His arrogant, meddling followers who have turned that message into one of privation and denial. And while I am not averse to playing with denial as a toy of pleasure, it can cause more harm than good when seen incorrectly."

19

George blinked, having no idea what the man was talking about.

"Thirdly," Potts continued, beginning to sound like some of the instructors George had endured as he'd earned his curate's collar, "if men like you would spend more time tending to the poor and the sick, as your friend Jesus admonished you all to do, and less time puffing up your own righteousness by pointing out motes in the eyes of others, this world would be a far finer place than it is."

A chill shot down George's spine. Potts was well-versed in the Bible, it seemed. But then, the Devil was a key character in the Word of God. He would have to know what he was talking about in order to desecrate it.

"And finally," Potts said, stroking George's calf in a way that was beginning to drive George to distraction, "to whom do you owe your duty besides your god? Clearly, someone else looms large in your imagination. Who is it?"

George's mouth dropped open at the directness of the question. The heat of embarrassment flushed through him as he thought about his answer. The very fact that his answer brought him shame was more than he wanted to think about. "Honor thy father" was something that had been quite literally beaten into him. So why did he feel like a worm admitting it?

No, he would not let this sinful devil steer him away from what he knew to be the straight and narrow path.

"My father," he said, tilting his chin up with pride. "My father has taught me everything I know. He has guided me through the pitfalls of life and shown me the way to preserve and protect my soul. It is my duty to share the pearl of wisdom he has given me, to continue his work above and beyond what he is capable of doing."

To George's surprise, Potts sighed and shook his head,

his shoulders dropping as though he were disappointed. Or as though he pitied George. "How old are you?" Potts asked him in a deceptively sweet and gentle voice.

"Five-and-twenty," George answered defiantly.

Potts's eyes went wide. "No!" he said. "You cannot be. You cannot be a day over twenty."

"Why would you say that?" George tried not to be offended, tried not to feel sheepish at the way Potts looked at him, as though he were less. He didn't want to be lesser in Potts's eyes. He wanted...he wanted to impress the man.

Potts laughed. The sound seemed to get under George's skin somehow. In all the time he'd spent doing his work outside of Perdition, waiting to catch a glimpse of its alluring owner, he'd never imagined Potts's laugh would sound so much like...like the thick, liquid chocolate he'd once indulged in.

"You're a year older than I," Potts said when he finished laughing. "I am four-and-twenty."

George's eyebrows flew up. "You cannot be," he said. "You own a gaming hell. You...you know how to tie me so I cannot get away."

He had no idea why he said the last bit, but he regretted it as soon as he did.

His words seemed to rekindle the fire in Potts. The man's face lit with wickedness, and with sudden, deft movements, he pushed away from the bedpost and moved to straddle George's waist and to lean over him. He planted his hands above George's arms, on either side of his head. The position brought their faces, their mouths to within inches of each other.

George suddenly couldn't catch his breath, particularly as Potts's movements bunched and pulled the blanket covering him so that it fell off his arms and exposed the upper part of his chest. The heat of Potts's body above his was nearly unbearable. Potts wore no neckcloth, and his shirt was unbuttoned enough to reveal a glimpse of his chest beneath.

"No," Potts said, nothing but wickedness in his eyes. "You cannot get away. You are mine now."

George squirmed against the shivers that raced through him at Potts's threat. He struggled in his bonds, tugging to get away. That only caused the parts of him that were close to Potts to brush against him and—God damn him—his cock to harden to the point where it tented the blanket covering him. He could only pray that Potts didn't notice, that his focus was on the terror in George's eyes and not his body's response to his captivity.

Except, George was no longer certain terror was what he felt. That was a part of it, but his emotions ran so wild that he couldn't hold on to any one of them. There were most definitely several enmeshed with his fear and indignation that he had never experienced before.

"Why?" he gasped, afraid to breathe too hard, lest Potts feel it against his lips. "What do you want from me?"

"What an interesting question," Potts purred. He balanced himself on one hand so that he could slowly, tantalizingly, pull the blanket that covered George lower and lower. "What do you have to give me?" he asked.

Potts tugged the blanket low enough to expose one of George's nipples. The brush of the fabric against that part of him was madly sensual. It shouldn't have been. Nipples on a man served no purpose. But that didn't stop George from wondering what it might feel like if Potts brought his mouth to that mound and sucked.

He let out a desperate sound, then immediately snapped his mouth shut in an attempt to drown it out.

What was wrong with him? What sort of wicked spell had Potts put on him.

"I just want to be good," he wailed, unable to control his response.

Immediately, he fell into the very depths of shame and despair. What kind of an idiot blurted out something like that with a predator perched atop him, trying to tempt him into sin?

He turned his head to the side, eyes squeezed shut, hoping he could disappear into the pillow. His father would sneer at him if he saw the levels to which he had sunk. As soon as he returned to his father's house, he would force himself to do penance—not the prayerful kind he was used to. He would, at last, take up his father's flogger and scourge his flesh for the betrayal it was committing now.

Except, it didn't feel like betrayal. It felt like chocolate, like wool and silk.

George fully expected Potts's hands to keep wandering, to touch him and wrench sensations from him that he had no wish to feel. No, that wasn't right. He wanted to feel them, even though he knew he shouldn't.

But Potts seemed to have frozen above him. The man didn't move at all. George could only feel his breath as it tickled his cheek.

Finally, after what felt like an agonizingly long moment of suspension, Potts said, "Age is not a matter of chronology. I am part owner of a gaming hell at the age of four-and-twenty because I worked for it. You know so little of the world at five-and-twenty because you have been sheltered from it."

George opened his eyes and twisted to stare up at Potts again. "I have seen much of the world," he argued in a whisper. "My father has taken me into the bowels of the city to spread the Gospel."

Potts shook his head...sadly. "You have seen things, but you have not lived them. I have. My mother raised me on her own, in the places where respectable people dared not go. She was a maid in a grand house, whose master trifled with her, and here I am. She was too proud to accept charity, or to make demands on my father, though he provided for her. Most gentlemen in that position do not, but my father genuinely cared for her. He visited me as well at least once a year, and he settled a sum on me when I reached my eighteenth year."

George blinked up at him. "So you...so you are not some criminal who was raised in the gutter? Someone who established this place through ill-gotten gains?"

Again, Potts laughed. "I am very much a criminal," he said, smiling in a way that had George's heart beating faster. "And those gains were ill-gotten, to an extent. If you consider charm and wiliness to be ill-gotten."

He shifted back a bit, sitting straighter. It gave George a better view of the man, but the way he sat, still straddling George's hips, brought their groins into very close proximity. And both of them were hard.

"My father liked me more and more the older I got, you see," Potts went on, seemingly proud of the fact. "I was his bastard, but I amused him to no end. More so than his legitimate heirs. I still do. We have become the unlikeliest of friends. It is he who enables Perdition to carry on, in spite of the rampant sin you disapprove of so vehemently."

"I—" George had nothing to follow that up with. He didn't know what to think now. Whoever Potts's natural father was, he must have been exceedingly powerful.

"And now, Rev. Mulgrew, you will answer my question," Potts said, sliding over George again. This time, the intent of their proximity was very clear. "What do you have to give me? I can offer a few suggestions, if you'd like."

He lowered his lips toward George's mouth, gazing teasingly into his eyes as he did. Every nerve and sinew in George's body vibrated with confusion. He should resist the Devil, resist temptation. His body was a traitor. It was hot and yearning, desperate to touch and be touched. He thanked God for the bonds that restricted him, then nearly laughed hysterically at that impetus to give thanks. He liked the way it felt to be bound and at Potts's mercy, because if he were unleashed, he feared what he would do.

"I'm waiting," Potts purred, his lips even closer to George's.

One of Potts's hands swept at the blanket, pulling it down to expose even more of him. George was afraid to look for fear that there was now a damp spot on the blanket between them.

He parted his lips to pant, his gaze fixed on Potts's eyes. How much would it cost him? How wicked would it be if he simply let Potts kiss him, let Potts caress him? Would God truly hold such pleasure and such mystery against him for all eternity if he let himself fall into it?

He teetered on the brink of giving up and letting himself fall when there was a knock at the door.

George tensed so hard that he let out a cry. Potts jerked as well, hissing and snapping straight.

Without so much as another knock, the door flew open, and an older man who George believed to be one of the club's other owners, stuck his head into the doorway. That man took one look at the position Potts and George were in, and the serious expression he wore flashed into mirth.

He laughed. "So this is what you intended when you

said you would take care of the good Rev. Mulgrew," he said, shaking his head. "My sincerest apologies for interrupting your communion."

"It had better be something important," Potts growled, breathing heavily. He didn't seem at all affected by being caught straddling a naked man in his bed, his erection straining hard against his breeches.

The other man's humor dropped. "It is, I'm afraid. Constance is in trouble. She needs you."

Chapter Three

Caesar pinched his face and swore colorfully enough to have Mulgrew blanching a little under him. The reaction was sweet, and it did nothing to calm the state of Caesar's ardor. Constance was important to him, though. She and the other residents of the downtrodden streets where he'd grown up were like his family, and he'd pledged to always be there when they needed him.

"I'll be along shortly," he told Jasper with a heavy sigh, dropping his head for a moment and sagging slightly over Mulgrew's still taut and bound body. And he had so been looking forward to seducing the curate and showing him another means of personal salvation.

"I'll ready a horse for you," Jasper said, still chuckling as he backed into the hall and shut the door.

Caesar grumbled, then took a moment to stare down at Mulgrew. The beautiful man wore a look of pure bafflement. His eyes were bright with lust and his face and neck were flushed, so whatever he said by way of protest for the position Caesar had him in, it would have been a lie.

"I must go sweetling," Caesar said, using the diminutive to play with Mulgrew. "I am needed elsewhere."

"Is Constance your...your wife?" Mulgrew asked.

Caesar laughed. "You think I have a wife?" he asked in return, then bent down to kiss Mulgrew's rosy lips. Mulgrew made a sound that wasn't quite a protest, his body going lax. Caesar grinned as he pulled up and gazed down at the stunned man. "Constance is a friend. One of many in the gutters where I grew up."

He climbed reluctantly off Mulgrew, sliding off the bed and moving to untie the man's feet.

"You would like those streets and alleys," he went on, since Mulgrew didn't seem to be in a mood for idle conversation. "They are all filled with just the sort of poor widows and orphans that your divine savior has told you to minister to."

"I—" Mulgrew started to protest, but didn't seem able to come up with an argument. Instead, he watched as Caesar untied his ankles, then circled the bed to untie his wrists as well.

"Rest assured," Caesar said, purposefully making his voice menacing with lust, "I will return to finish what we have begun here."

He untied Mulgrew's second wrist, effectively freeing him, but before letting the man's hand go, he turned it over to kiss Mulgrew's palm, to run his tongue across it, and to draw two of the man's fingers into his mouth to suck on them. Mulgrew drew in a shuddering breath, and Caesar was gratified to see the tent he'd made of the thin blanket covering him was pitched as high as ever.

He chuckled, then released Mulgrew's hand and stepped back. "Until I return, love. My house is your home."

He sent Mulgrew one last, deeply wicked look, then

headed for the door. He stepped into the hallway without looking back. When he shut the door, he deliberately didn't lock it. He was curious to see whether Mulgrew would make a run for it or whether he was tempted into staying until Caesar returned.

There was no telling how long his mission would take, however. If Constance had called for him, that meant there was trouble that she could not resolve on her own, which was never a good or easy thing. Caesar attempted to forget about Mulgrew lying naked in his bed as he fetched his jacket from his office, sorted his appearance, then headed out to the mews to fetch the horse Jasper had prepared for him.

The streets and alleys where Caesar had been raised were not in the very bowels of London, like some of his friends had come from. His natural father had cared for his mother enough to set her up in a reasonable situation, though his mother had been proud from the start and reticent to accept too much help. Besides, it wouldn't have been seemly for a disgraced maid to live in a Mayfair townhouse.

The streets where Caesar had spent his formative years were a bit rough, but the people there meant well, and he truly did feel it was his responsibility to ensure order was kept and his friends and former neighbors were able to pursue their lives and livelihoods in peace.

Mulgrew truly would have been proud of the order that had been wrought from the chaos of poverty and uncertainty. Or so Caesar thought with a smile as he rode past the boundaries of respectable London and into the more questionable part of town. His status in that part of the city, his intimidating appearance in spite of his age, and the almost dreamy smile he wore as he headed on to his destination kept him from being accosted by the waifs and vagrants that dotted the area.

Mulgrew was a treat Caesar hadn't expected to be handed that morning. He'd had no idea such a fierce and passionate heart beat under the drab and irritating exterior of the curate. The man could rail against sin and claim to be saving souls all he wanted, but there had been something else in the depths of his dark eyes. He could have shouted at Caesar and thrown insults and damnation at him upon waking in another man's bed and finding himself bound and naked, but Mulgrew had remained relatively passive about his situation.

And what a beautiful situation it was. The blanket had been mostly to maintain Mulgrew's modesty when he awoke. Caesar had already drunk his fill of the sight of the man's body while undressing him and fastening him in his bonds in the first place. Despite the threadbare and misshapen clothing Mulgrew wore, he had a fit and shapely body that was made for sin. Caesar had been desperately tempted to stroke and explore all of it, once he'd had Mulgrew tied and stretched for his pleasure.

The man's cock had been particularly intriguing because of its size. If that was what Mulgrew looked like flaccid, Caesar burned to get a look at him when he was fully aroused. His arsehole twitched at the thought of what Mulgrew's hard prick would feel like buried deep inside him.

Caesar was forced to take a deep breath to clear those thoughts and to settle his eager body as he rode right into the scene of chaos Constance must have called him to alleviate. He would have time to contemplate all the ways he would order Mulgrew to fuck him senseless as soon as his business in his old neighborhood was completed.

Ahead, several doors down the street, Constance was doing her best to shelter a timid, willowy woman from a thick brute of a man who seemed intent on going after her.

"I told you to stay away, Roger, and I meant it," Constance growled at him as the woman cowered behind her. "You've raised a hand to Nancy for the last time."

That was all Caesar needed to hear. He abhorred men who thought they had a right to beat or abuse women in any way. He might not have resided on his old street anymore, but he knew enough about its current inhabitants to recall that Roger was Nancy's husband, and that he was addicted to gin.

"She's my wife," Roger shouted, his words slurred, as Caesar dismounted, handed his horse off to one of the lads who rushed forward and gazed at him with awe in his eyes, then strode straight for the odious man. "I can do whatever I damn well please to her."

"You can," Caesar said, stepping right into the fray and grabbing Roger by the back of his collar. "But you'll have to face me if you do it."

Roger was already soused, which made him slow to react as Caesar yanked him back sharply. Roger made a sound of muddled confusion, then his eyes went wide as he recognized who had him.

"Would you care to explain to me why I have been called away from a perfectly pleasant morning to intervene in this matter?" Caesar asked the brute with deceptive calm.

"Oh, er, Potts," Roger stammered, twisting in an attempt to get away from Caesar's iron grip. "She's my wife," he argued, if such a statement could even be called an argument. "She ain't been doing her duty by me."

"Not while he's drunk," Nancy said in a frightened

31

voice from behind Constance. "He's...he's mean when he's drunk."

That statement could have covered a myriad of evils that Caesar was loath to think about.

"Do you want this husband of yours?" he asked Nancy. "Do you want to keep him?"

"Hang on," Roger asked, beginning to catch on to the situation he found himself in.

Nancy gulped as she stared at Roger, then peeked at Caesar and shook her head before hiding fully behind Constance.

"I believe that settles that matter," Caesar said. He pushed Roger away, causing the man to stumble. "You will leave London by nightfall. If you're ever seen on these streets or anywhere near poor Nancy here, well, that will be the last time you are seen, if I make myself clear."

Roger gaped at him. "You cannot...I will not be...you wouldn't really do that, would you?" he asked at last, blinking blearily.

"You could always stay and test me," Caesar said with a shrug.

Evidently, that was intimidation enough for Roger. He made a sound that didn't quite form words, then turned and lurched away. After a few unsteady steps, he broke into a jog. A few moments later, he disappeared around the streetcorner.

"Let me know if he accosts you again, Nancy," he told the woman as she peeked over Constance's shoulder. Nancy nodded.

"Many thanks, Caesar," Constance told Caesar with a relieved smile. "I wouldn't have called for you, but Roger has been threatening Nancy here with much worse for a while. What you did just now was exactly what needed to be done."

Caesar smiled, walking over to kiss his old friend on her cheek. "Do you think he'll stay away, or shall I have Davy alerted he might have a job awaiting him?" he asked.

Constance pinched her face, then said with a sigh, "Alert Davy. I don't think Roger will wander off without encouragement." She gave Caesar a pointed look.

Caesar laughed grimly and glanced past Constance to Nancy. "Will you be alright?" he asked her.

Nancy nodded tightly. "Yes, sir. Thank you, sir." She even dipped a quick curtsy before turning and running, as if she were as afraid of him as Roger had been.

Caesar chuckled at that, then glanced to Constance again. "Do you need me for anything else?" he asked. "I've a rather pressing matter back at the club to deal with." Seduction was always a pressing matter...if Mulgrew stayed where he was instead of fleeing at the first opportunity.

Constance frowned in thought. "To be honest, Caesar, I could use your help feeding some of this rabble."

"Oh?" Caesar met her serious concern with his own.

Constance sighed. "More and more of them keep coming in from the country. It's getting so we can't find places for them all, or jobs. I hate to ask for more than you already give, but if you could spare a few loaves of bread, perhaps some sturdy clothes and shoes, and if any of them seem the sort who might come and work for you, in whatever capacity, I'd appreciate your assistance."

A spark of an idea came to Caesar's mind. The sort of help Constance was asking for was precisely the kind of thing Mulgrew needed to see.

"I will send something tonight and come by tomorrow,"

he said, smiling at his idea as it gained speed. "I might just bring a friend along with me," he added.

"Any friend of yours is always welcome here," Constance said.

They said their goodbyes, and Caesar went back to fetch his horse, flicking a coin to the lad who had held him the whole time. He mounted and started eagerly back to St. James's, though he had an errand he needed to run first. His mind was already set on what he wanted, however, and he was willing to wager that a visit to his old haunts would be precisely how he could win that.

The situation George found himself in as soon as Potts departed was eerie, to say the least. He'd been freed from the silken cord that had bound him to Potts's bed—though the cord itself had been left wrapped around his wrists and ankles, as if to be some sort of reminder of his captivity—but he remained naked. And aroused. That small detail filled him with guilt and shame...and other, hotter emotions that he absolutely refused to think about.

He waited for a long time before so much as moving on the bed. Potts's departure could have been a ploy, for all he knew. The devil could simply be waiting for him to lower his guard and uncover himself before leaping back into the room and pouncing on him. He could be lingering, waiting for the chance to press his body against George's and to capture his lips in another searing kiss that would adle his brain, like that first, painfully short and shallow kiss had.

George raised a hand to his lips, remembering the way Potts's had felt against his own. He'd never been kissed by a man before. He'd never been kissed by anyone. Not so much as a peck on the cheek by his long-deceased mother as a show of affection. He'd no idea something as simple as two mouths touching each other could elicit such vibrant feelings through his entire body.

His cock jumped at the memory of Potts's kiss, and as soon as it did, George scowled. He could not travel down the wide path in such a way. Lust was a sin. Sins of the flesh were the very worst kind. He could not fall prey to their allure, not for any reason.

He threw off the blanket, determined to search the room for more suitable clothing to cover his shame. Of course, the sight of his engorged prick standing against his hip as he rolled to the side did nothing to ease the desire pulsing through him. He shouldn't have taken such pleasure in looking at his own body's rebelliousness, but all he could think about was what Potts might think of the way he looked.

He cursed himself as he scrambled off the bed, pulling at the silken cords on his wrists until he removed them and let the cords slither to the floor. He did the same with the silk around his ankles, then stepped away from the pile around him as though it were made of snakes instead of rope.

His first priority was to clothe himself. He was in a bedroom, there was a wardrobe staring right at him from the other side of the room, and Potts was relatively close to him in size, so he wagered that would be the easiest of his tasks. Indeed, as soon as he threw open the wardrobe doors, he was faced with a startling number of clean shirts, breeches in several colors, at least a dozen waistcoats, and every other accoutrement of fine fashion that he could wish for.

For a moment, George merely stared at it all. Then he reached up to stroke his hands over the cool, crisp linen and cotton of Potts's shirts. He couldn't remember the last time he'd seen such finery or felt soft fabric like that. His father certainly could have afforded comfortable clothing for George and for himself, but he was forever preaching against the dangers of worldly things.

Still, something close to longing stirred in George's chest as he studied the contents of Potts's wardrobe. He knew that gaming hells were profitable enterprises, if they were managed correctly and stayed away from the law. He'd had no idea Perdition made the sort of profit that enabled Potts to dress like a prince, though.

It was just a bit too much for George to think about, so instead of rushing to clothe himself in borrowed finery, he moved to the washstand off to one side of the room. Cleansing his body would certainly cleanse his mind and leave him better equipped to resist temptation.

But Potts's soap held a beautiful fragrance of lemons, and George enjoyed washing himself with it far more than he felt he should have. Potts's shaving soap was similarly fragrant, though it tickled his nose with exotic spices and whispers of adventures in bright, foreign places as he drew the razor over his jaw.

By the time he was clean and smooth, sense seemed to return to George, and he frowned at himself. The pleasures of the flesh were seductive indeed. He couldn't remember the last time he'd smelled so fresh or felt so clean...while simultaneously feeling dirty. He cursed himself silently, recited a few of the Bible verses his father had pounded into his head, and returned to the wardrobe to dress in the simplest of Potts's clothing that he could find.

They fit reasonably well, which didn't settle right with George. His legs were a bit thicker than Potts's, which made the breeches skin-tight, but Potts had broader shoulders, which meant his shirt and waistcoat were a touch too large.

He admired the way he looked in a tall mirror that stood in the corner...and he couldn't help but wonder who the man that stared back at him from that mirror could have been, had he not been raised under the thumb of a father intent on saving souls.

Those thoughts were too much to contemplate, so George moved away from the mirror and surveyed the room. What he truly needed was some sort of evidence of Potts's evil, something he could take to the Bow Street runners to incriminate Potts and the whole of Perdition. If he could find receipts for wrongdoing, books that accounted for bribery, embezzlement, or illegal speculations, then he could bring the hell he found himself in down around Potts's feet.

Something about that idea didn't sit well with George, but he ignored the feeling and set to work, opening drawers in the wardrobe and the chest of drawers and table beside Potts's bed. His face flushed hot as he found a jar of something slick in the table beside the bed, along with a few thick, protuberant items of wood and marble that bore an uncomfortable resemblance to phalluses.

His heart was racing fast over that discovery, and the speed with which he'd slammed the drawer shut and fled to the other side of the room, when he found precisely what he was looking for in a carved box sitting on the mantelpiece of the fireplace. The box contained dozens of envelopes, correspondence from Potts's wicked deeds, no doubt. George took the box to the chair by the window and set to work reading the letters, bristling with excitement over the damning evidence he was certain they would contain.

But the first letter was from the Sisters of Mercy, thanking Potts and blessing him for a generous contribution he had made to fund their orphanage on the Isle of Dogs.

The second he read was more thanks from a similar organization that took in children who had been abandoned by their indigent parents. Potts hadn't just given them money. Apparently, he gave a great deal of his time to educating those young people and searching out honest employment for them.

The next six letters held more of the same. Potts gave copiously of his time and his treasure to those less fortunate than him. The box was filled with thanks and praise from people who had been saved from starvation, abuse, and, ironically, prostitution.

It didn't make a lick of sense to George. Potts was the devil. He knew that to be true. He operated a gaming hell, employed prostitutes himself, and engaged in every sort of wickedness. The man had captured him and kept him naked and tied to a bed. He'd almost molested George—though just thinking about it had George aching with unspent passion all over again—and Potts had locked him in a room, refusing to let him go.

It couldn't be possible that his kidnapper and gaoler was the same man that the letters—which had spilled across the table by the chair where George sat in the hour or so that it took him to read through them all—praised for his generosity and grace.

Nothing made sense anymore. Not one single thing. And he didn't know what to do about it. He had no idea how to reconcile the things he'd witnessed for himself and the story the letters in front of him told. It was as if—

That thought was cut short as the bedchamber door opened without warning and Potts himself stepped into the room. He glanced to the bed at first, then searched and found George sitting, surrounded by letters. The smile that burst across Potts's face at the sight of him had George's body in full rebellion all over again.

"Well, don't you look a treat, dressed in my things like that," Potts said, shutting the door behind him and stalking toward George.

George realized two things almost at once. Potts hadn't unlocked the door before coming in, which meant it had never been locked in the first place. He could have walked out of the room, out of Perdition, any time he'd wanted to.

His second realization was that he didn't want to.

Chapter Four

The sight that met Caesar when he returned to his bedchamber left him breathless and excited. Mulgrew was still there. The delicious man hadn't fled in terror. Not only that, he'd cleaned himself up and dressed in Caesar's clothes. He'd even shaved, which filled Caesar with the urge to caress and kiss the man's smooth face.

Perhaps best of all was the startled flush that painted Mulgrew's face as the man was caught red-handed reading Caesar's correspondence. Caesar knew full well what those letters contained. Mulgrew knew now as well, and the dumbfounded, almost pleading look the man wore was all the proof needed that his dear curate had just had his view of the world upended.

Well, Caesar couldn't have that. Mulgrew needed to see him as the sinner and himself as the saint. Anything less would upset the man a bit too much, possibly causing him to run. And the very last thing Caesar wanted now, particularly with his prisoner looking as fetching as he did, was for Mulgrew to run.

"You've made a mess of my correspondence," he said as he approached Mulgrew with all the sly grace of a predator. "My *personal* correspondence."

"I...I'm sorry," Mulgrew said. A beat passed, then he began attempting to hastily stuff the array of envelopes and letters scattered across the table, the chair, and his lap, into their box.

It was darling of him, really. Mulgrew was a precious gem of a man. He felt so much younger than Caesar, even though he'd admitted to being a year older.

Caesar stepped all the way over to the chair, planted his hands on the arms with enough force to make Mulgrew jump and drop the letters he'd just picked up, and leaned into the man. Mulgrew plastered himself against the back of the chair as Caesar drew in a breath, sniffing the scents of his soap, shaving soap, and Mulgrew himself. He drew his nose up over the curve of Mulgrew's neck until his lips nearly touched his ear.

"You smell good enough to eat," he whispered, then flicked out his tongue to tease Mulgrew's earlobe.

Mulgrew flinched, then let out the most delectable sigh Caesar had ever heard. His dear curate might have dedicated his life to God, but he was a fruit ripe for the Devil's picking, and Caesar reveled in his role as the Devil.

He leaned back and set to work gathering the remainder of his letters from Mulgrew's lap—which, of course, allowed him to come as close to touching and caressing all of Mulgrew's important parts without actually molesting him.

"Did you read anything interesting?" he asked, one eyebrow arched. "Anything...edifying?"

Mulgrew schooled his expression into a light frown. "You know I did," he said with surprising calm. He paused as Caesar took the box of letters back to the mantel, then said, "I trust those letters are not forgeries or fakes."

Caesar laughed at the idea. "No, they are not. I should be offended that you would even dream of such a thing."

He glanced over his shoulder as Mulgrew squirmed in his seat.

"I am sorry," he murmured, staring guiltily at Caesar's back.

No, not his back, his arse. Caesar grinned from ear to ear, taking his time as he settled the box back in place and arching in a way that gave Mulgrew more to look at. Seducing the curate would be child's play.

"I bought you a little something while I was out," he said, turning away from the mantel and striding back to Mulgrew.

Mulgrew blinked up at him. "You...bought me something?"

Caesar's grin widened as he reached inside of his jacket, where he'd tucked the gift. "Indeed." Slowly, he pulled out a long, cream-colored silk neckcloth. Once he'd removed it from his jacket, he leaned forward to drape it around Mulgrew's neck. He used it to pull the man forward. "How convenient that you left off a neckcloth while donning my clothing this morning."

Caesar let his gaze drop to the hint of skin that was visible under the loosely fastened collar of Mulgrew's shirt.

"I didn't mean—" Mulgrew started, but didn't seem to know where those words were intended to take him.

"I know," Caesar said, though it felt like something nonsensical instead of an actual statement of knowledge.

He let the ends of the neckcloth drop and planted his hands on the arms of the chair again. Even though he'd just pulled Mulgrew forward, he leaned into him, nudging him back, until Mulgrew had nowhere to go. Instead of teasing him, Caesar pressed right into him, slanting his mouth over Mulgrew's and stealing the kiss he'd dreamed about the entire time he'd spent searching for a gift for Mulgrew on Oxford Street.

Mulgrew gasped, which only served to open his mouth enough for Caesar to invade with his tongue. Once that barrier was crossed, Mulgrew moaned and went limp against the back of the chair. It was their second kiss and the second time the man had appeared to go boneless at the simple, intimate contact. It was immediately clear that Mulgrew didn't know the first thing about kissing—and why would he, given the little Caesar knew about his stilted, sin-averse life—but it was also clear he was starving for affection.

Caesar tried not to let the implications of that anger him. Without knowing much at all, he firmly placed the blame at Mulgrew's father's feet. A man like George Mulgrew should be kissed often and lavished with affection. He drank up Caesar's kiss as though it were the first rain after decades of drought.

Similarly to that morning, a knock at the door interrupted the moment of pleasure just as Caesar was warming up. This time, however, he knew what the interruption was about, and the maid he knew was waiting in the hall did not burst in like Jasper Black had.

"Just a moment, love," Caesar murmured against Mulgrew's mouth. "I have something else for you."

He kissed Mulgrew's lips quickly, then pushed back and marched across the room. He took particular care with the way he walked as well, figuring Mulgrew was staring at his arse again.

Sarah, one of Perdition's kitchen maids, waited on the

other side of the door with the tray bearing afternoon tea that Caesar had requested before returning to his bedchamber. Caesar took it from her and thanked her with a wink. Sarah was a good, sharp-witted girl, one of the ones he'd taken from the street on Constance's suggestion and given gainful employment. Perdition wasn't all evil, as he was intent on proving to Mulgrew.

"I take it you are a might peckish?" he said, carrying the tray to the small table beside the chair where Mulgrew seemed frozen in shock. Seeing that shock, Caesar made it a point to pretend to be as casual as possible. "I see Sarah has prepared a bit of savory along with the sweet. She is such a clever girl to recognize we have both skipped luncheon. Do you care if I pour?"

It was simply too amusing to blindside Mulgrew with kindness, but perhaps it was also a bit too much.

"I...I must go," Mulgrew said, sliding forward and attempting to stand.

Caesar cursed himself for laying it on too thick, too quickly. He stepped in front of Mulgrew and placed a hand against the man's chest to push him back into the chair.

"Perhaps I have not made myself clear," he said, a wicked grin pulling at the corners of his kiss-warmed lips. "I *insist* you join me for tea." He made his tone as dark and amorous as he could.

"I cannot," Mulgrew said, wriggling as he tried to find the leverage to stand again. "I shouldn't be here," he went on. "This place, you...it is sinful. I cannot let myself be led astray."

"Why not?" Caesar asked, smiling down at his darling curate. "What is so very wrong with being led astray? At least when one is being led, he is not alone."

Mulgrew blinked at that answer and snapped his mouth

shut. He stared up at Caesar for a moment before saying, "The way of Truth is clear. The path of righteousness is...."

Caesar waited a moment, letting Mulgrew's thoughts, whatever they may have been, take his words. It was charming to see a man lose the strength of his conviction when he was faced with a greater and more beautiful truth.

"The path of the righteous does not necessarily lead to Paradise," he said at last, when Mulgrew looked desperate for help. He brushed his fingertips around Mulgrew's face as he did. "And those who profess to follow God and to do His will are not always the ones doing it. But I think you have come to understand this by now."

Mulgrew remained silent, staring up at Caesar as though deeply conflicted.

Caesar made a decision then. He wasn't entirely certain he was reading Mulgrew right, but he was willing to take a gamble on what he needed to do to secure the man's happiness and to open his world to everything the man so obviously wanted, but had denied himself.

"Very well," he said, taking a half step back and grabbing the neckcloth he'd given Mulgrew. "If you will not join me for tea the easy way, if you insist on being my prisoner instead of my guest, then I will treat you as such."

"I beg your pardon?"

Mulgrew was barely able to get the question past his lips when Caesar yanked the neckcloth from around his shoulders, pulled him forward and bent him double at the waist, then grasped his arms and forced them behind his back. Mulgrew was so startled by the action that he barely struggled as Caesar used the newly-purchased neckcloth to tie Mulgrew's wrists together. He fastened the bonds as tightly as he could, checking to make certain Mulgrew's circulation was not affected, then pulled on Mulgrew's shoulders until he sat straight again.

Mulgrew let out a few panting breaths, his eyes wide as he came to grips with what Caesar had just done. "I cannot —" he started, tugging at his bound wrists behind him.

Caesar waited with bated breath for a moment, pretending nonchalance when he was actually bristling with nervousness to see if he'd gone too far. He wanted to tease and tempt Mulgrew into staying, and instinct told him the man would be far more willing to let himself be led off his narrow path if he was given the illusion of having no choice in the matter.

Within seconds, Caesar could see the gamble had paid off. Mulgrew only tugged at his wrists for a moment before letting out a heavy breath and slumping with defeat. It was a curious sort of defeat though—one that seemed to enliven the man and put a spark in his eyes that begged Caesar to fan it. It would have been easy for Mulgrew to free himself. A silk neckcloth could not hold a man intent on escape for long. But Mulgrew's attempts to escape were feeble and short-lived.

Caesar loved it. He stepped away to pull another chair over, then sat right in front of Mulgrew, their knees touching.

"Now," he said, turning his attention to the tea. "Do you take cream and sugar or lemon?"

Mulgrew was silent for a long time before mumbling, "Cream and sugar."

"Very good," Caesar said with a nod. As he poured, he did his best imitation of his mother when she was feeling particularly lofty, then added the cream and sugar. "Tell me if this is to your liking," he said.

It was nearly impossible to keep a straight face as he

held the teacup to Mulgrew's lips, then waited for the man to stare incredulously at him for a moment before making a move to drink. Caesar tipped the cup just enough for Mulgrew to drink his fill, and when the man pulled away and swallowed, Caesar raised one eyebrow in question.

Mulgrew blinked at him, then belatedly said, "It is very good, thank you."

"Another?" Caesar asked, moving the teacup back to his lips.

Mulgrew looked as though he'd fallen into some sort of mad dream, but he inched forward to accept another sip of tea.

"Shall we try some of these delicious savory tarts Cook has prepared?" Caesar asked. He drank from Mulgrew's cup, then set it back on the tray, picking up one of the tarts instead.

Mulgrew gaped a bit as Caesar held out the tart to him. "Are you...are you going to feed me the entire tea?" he asked, more than a bit breathless.

"I don't see how you could feed yourself at this point," Caesar said, his lips twitching with mirth as he nodded to one side, where Mulgrew's arm disappeared behind his back.

"You could untie me," Mulgrew suggested, the faintest flash of challenge in his eyes.

Caesar took a bite of the tart, chewed it with a smile, then swallowed. "No, I think not," he said, offering Mulgrew the tart again. "You enjoy being restrained too much."

"I...I do not," Mulgrew said, his face going bright red. He darted forward and snapped a bit of the tart—which felt to Caesar like a contradiction of his words. Mulgrew could

47

pretend all he wanted, but he was enjoying the game they were playing.

Caesar waited until his curate had swallowed his bite, then offered him another. Mulgrew ate, and Caesar popped the remainder of the tart into his own mouth.

"What do you think?" he asked. "Should Cook continue with this recipe, or should she discard it in favor of something a bit tastier?"

"I—" Mulgrew blinked at him. "It is finer than the fare I usually eat."

That both intrigued and infuriated Caesar. "What do you usually eat?" he asked, reaching for the teacup once more.

He took a swallow himself, then offered it to Mulgrew. Mulgrew drank, inching back when he'd had enough. Caesar took another sip, then set the cup down to pick up another savory tart.

"My father insists simple fare is enough to nourish the body, and that the soul requires nothing more than a steady diet of scripture," Mulgrew said at last.

Caesar snorted and scoffed. "Lies. God does not wish for us to be miserable. He created choice cuts of meat, butter, garlic, and spices so that we might enjoy His creation with all our senses."

That statement startled Mulgrew. As he gaped, Caesar took a bite of the fresh tart, then held it out for his sweetheart.

It felt like a poignant victory when Mulgrew leaned in to take a bite without putting up a moment of resistance or fuss. "My father would argue that the Devil put those things before us to tempt us away from the righteous path," he said.

Caesar laughed. Mulgrew's eyes sparkled at the sound.

Caesar gestured for Mulgrew to take another bite of the tart, then finished it himself.

"It almost sounds as though your father believes the Devil to be far more powerful than God," he said with his mouth full. "Is that what you believe, Rev. Mulgrew? Or do you simply follow your father's path because no better way has been shown to you?"

The comment was intended to be teasing, but the shame and grief that came into Mulgrew's eyes was anything but.

"My father has raised me and provided for me my whole life," Mulgrew said, glancing down as if he couldn't meet Caesar's eyes. "He has shown me the way of God, the one true way to Heaven."

"Has he?" Caesar asked gently, his heart breaking for Mulgrew. He took another drink of tea, then offered the cup to Mulgrew.

Mulgrew drank a sip, then shook his head. "There is only one true way to the Father, and that is through His son."

Caesar winced at those words. They held far too much agony for any profession of faith.

He put the cup down and scooted forward, his knees wedged between Mulgrew's. "Let me show you a different path to Paradise," he whispered, stroking his hands up Mulgrew's sides to cup his face.

He leaned in, slanting his mouth over Mulgrew's and giving his passion free rein. Mulgrew sucked in a breath, then let it out with a shudder. He parted his lips, not only allowing Caesar to kiss him, but inviting him in. It was sweet and poignant, and it was made even more so by the desperation to be loved that Caesar felt pouring off the man. Mulgrew was so ready to be loved that it took every ounce of patience Caesar had not to simply pounce on him and take what he wanted.

He did want it, though, and Caesar always got what he wanted. He stood, drawing Mulgrew up with him, and nudged his chair back so that he could draw Mulgrew toward the bed.

"I am going to untie your hands," he purred, never taking his hands off Mulgrew's face or peeling his eyes away from his. "Once you are unbound, you are free to leave, if that is what you want. But if you don't flee my presence, I am going to strip you naked again, and myself, and I am going to take you to my bed and show you a world of pleasure and affection that you have never imagined. The choice is yours."

Mulgrew didn't answer with words. His chest rose and fell in shallow pants. His eyes were glassy and fixed on Caesar's. The need that radiated from him was like the heat of the first fire on a cold day. But the real test was yet to come.

Caesar led him halfway across the room, then dropped his hands, sweeping them over Mulgrew's body, as he walked around to undo the neckcloth from Mulgrew's wrists. He could feel Mulgrew trembling as he picked through the loose knot he'd made and untied the silk. Caesar let it side gently over Mulgrew's skin before dropping the silk to the floor. Before he walked around to face Mulgrew again, he tugged his shirt out of the waist of his breeches, then slid his hands along the bare flesh of Mulgrew's side and stomach.

"Are you frightened?" Caesar asked, pressing his chest against Mulgrew's back and his growing erection against Mulgrew's arse.

Mulgrew nodded tightly. That bit of honesty shot straight to Caesar's heart.

He stroked Mulgrew's stomach for a moment before lowering his hands to undo the fall of Mulgrew's breeches. All he did was undo them and let them sag. The temptation to fondle Mulgrew's cock and balls was almost irresistible, but he wanted to be absolutely certain it was what his darling curate wanted first.

Instead, he swept his hands back up Mulgrew's taut and quivering stomach and across his chest to play with his nipples. Mulgrew let out a vocal sigh that turned into a pleading whimper.

Caesar leaned close to his ear and murmured, "Are you going to run away?"

Mulgrew took a few gulping breaths, then shook his head.

Caesar smiled and laughed sensually against the crook of Mulgrew's neck. He was rewarded with a shiver that he felt pass through Mulgrew's entire body. "I knew you would stay," he said, then brushed his hands down Mulgrew's body.

Now he knew his love was ready. He dipped his hands into Mulgrew's breeches, scooping up the man's balls with one hand and sliding the other along the length of his hard cock to stroke it free of the confining fabric. Mulgrew moaned, and for a moment, he went heavy in Caesar's arms as his knees gave out.

"Shh, shh, darling," Caesar whispered, nibbling Mulgrew's neck. "I have you."

Caesar moved as swiftly as he could while maintaining the aura of sensuality they'd found themselves in. He was well aware this was Mulgrew's first time, which meant he wouldn't last more than a few minutes, if that. He wanted his darling's first orgasm with a partner to pleasure them both, and since he knew full well what he liked, he maneuvered Mulgrew onto the bed on his back.

He made quick work of the clothing Mulgrew wore, undressing him and himself haphazardly and throwing their clothes wherever they might land. He was sure to retrieve the jar he kept in his bedside table before throwing back the bedcovers and nestling him and Mulgrew on the cool sheets. The contrast of hot and cold left Caesar shivering in more ways than one, but it was the sight of Mulgrew lying in a position of sensual surrender in his bed that had Caesar breathing hard and the tip of his cock leaking with want.

Mulgrew was too beautiful a sight to resist. His skin was flushed with desire, and his nipples were pert with expectation. Caesar straddled him as he had that morning, but with nothing impeding the rub of skin against skin. It felt so good that he let out a groan and indulged in it for a moment, grinding his hard cock against Mulgrew's. Mulgrew gasped and moaned, his hips flexing instinctively.

Caesar laughed deep in his throat. "No, you aren't going to last long, are you love?" He could already feel the wild tension coiled in Mulgrew's body.

"I don't know how—" Mulgrew panted, his face pinching in distress. "I want to...but I don't know—"

Caesar grinned as he bent forward, touching his lips briefly to Mulgrew's. "Just this once, I'll do all the work. But in future, I expect you to put everything you have into pleasuring me." He grasped Mulgrew's hands and pulled them up to pin them above Mulgrew's head. "Do you think you can do that for me?" he purred, stealing another kiss. "Can you give it all to me? Because I like to be taken hard and rough." He kissed Mulgrew again, noting that his love could barely catch his breath and that his eyes had gone glassy.

"Would you like to fuck me hard, Reverend? Do you think you could fuck the devil out of me?"

Caesar sensed he'd gone a bit too far by the way Mulgrew groaned and writhed under him. His love jerked his hips as though Nature was showing him exactly how to fulfill Caesar's filthy request. It boded well for their future, once Mulgrew had learned some control and mastery of his own body. As soon as the man was capable of obeying Caesar's commands not to come until he wanted it, there was no end to the pleasure they could find together.

That thought had him halfway to orgasm himself. He pushed himself up, reached for the jar, and pulled out the cork so he could scoop its contents onto his fingers. As Mulgrew watched, aroused and perplexed, Caesar slicked his helpless curate's hard, thick cock, then reached behind to spread the remainder over his hole. He fingered himself while he was at it, and when he was satisfied that Mulgrew's massive cock would give him the right sort of pain, he moved into position.

It would have been easier to ask Mulgrew to hold his own cock up, but that would have defeated the purpose of shocking his love with pleasure he didn't know he was in for. Caesar did the honors himself, twisting awkwardly until the head of Mulgrew's cock pressed against his hole, then bearing down on him.

Mulgrew let out a sound like Caesar had never heard and his eyes went wide as Caesar sheathed him. Caesar moaned with the pleasure of it himself, pumping Mulgrew deeper and deeper until he was fully lodged within him. Everything about the joining was perfect bliss. Mulgrew's size was punishing, but Caesar loved it.

He gave Mulgrew only a few seconds to adjust to the new sensation before moving, drawing him out and in again, and adjusting his angle until that massive cock hit him perfectly. Once he found the right position and rhythm, Caesar let go. He fucked himself as hard as he dared, balancing with one hand on the bed while his other stroked his cock. Mulgrew wasn't going to last long, but he didn't want to either. He wanted them both to come as close together as possible.

He could tell by the increasing intensity of the sounds Mulgrew made that he was close, and when those sounds turned into a protracted cry as Mulgrew jerked his hips hard on instinct, spilling himself inside of Caesar, Caesar couldn't wait another second. He levered himself up so that he could watch Mulgrew's contorted face as his orgasm slowed and abated, then stroked his cock furiously until he also burst. He sent thick ribbons of seed across Mulgrew's stomach and chest, making the man into the most beautiful work of art in the entire house.

The moment was perfect and exhilarating, and it passed all too soon. Exhausted, Caesar slumped over his darling, kissing his panting mouth and twining their tongues together as their bodies were still joined. That took too much effort to maintain, though, so he gingerly slid off of Mulgrew before collapsing to his side. The two of them were overheated and sweaty, and his seed was sticky between them, but that didn't stop him from pulling Mulgrew into his arms and kissing him again.

"Paradise," he gasped when he regained the last bit of his sanity. "Just as I promised."

Mulgrew made one last delicious, helpless sound before his eyes fluttered closed and he fell asleep.

Chapter Five

The Devil was indeed persuasive.

George didn't think he'd ever slept so deeply or rested so profoundly in his life. He had not ever been surrounded by so much comfort, for one. Caesar's bed was thick and soft, and the sheets and coverings were made of the finest linens. For another, he hadn't gone to bed hungry. After tea, later in the evening, Caesar had served him a generous supper, one that was almost too heavy for his palate. It had given George a new appreciation of what it felt like to go to bed with a full belly.

But those were not the true reasons he had slept like the dead. The true reason George had slept so soundly was because he had been thoroughly worn out in body and soul.

He stretched carefully as sleep left him with the first light of dawn, feeling the strain of muscles he'd never used in that particular way the night before. Memories of everything he'd done to earn those strains rushed in on him as he felt the cool slip of the sheets around him and the softness of the pillow under his head.

His whole body flushed as he corrected himself. The

memories didn't come from the feel of the sheets or pillows, they came from the warm, hard body beside him, cradling him. They came from the naked form of Caesar Potts as he slumbered on with one arm draped over George's side, holding George's back against his chest.

The urge not only to stretch but to writhe and rub himself against Caesar, like a cat staking its claim to a spot of sunlight, was almost irresistible. It was wickedness incarnate—*Caesar* was wickedness incarnate. He had tempted and seduced George relentlessly from the moment he'd returned to the bedchamber and caught George reading his correspondence. He had stripped George and left him bare in far more ways than just removing his clothing.

They had sinned together. Wickedly. *Deeply.*

George sucked in a breath, stifling the moan that wanted to escape him at that deceptively simple word. It was no longer innocent. It conjured to mind the sight of his erect cock sinking deeply into Caesar's arse, all the way to the hilt, as the man groaned and strained, his face contorted in a look of ecstasy, his whole body—

George clenched his jaw and squeezed his eyes shut, trying to force the image away. He couldn't rid himself of the memory of what it had felt like to have his throbbing member enclosed and squeezed until he went half mad with need. Part of him had been deeply ashamed to spill his seed inside of Caesar—not just once, either. Caesar had demanded that sinful invasion and release from him twice more in the evening and night, before they'd fallen asleep. And God help him, George had given it gladly.

Yes, part of him felt guilty. The rest of him had soared with pleasure and excitement, and even some sort of communion with Caesar that had bordered on fondness.

"You are entirely too tense for lazing about in bed of a

morning with your lover," Caesar's voice murmured against George's ear, causing him to gasp and jerk in surprise.

"I did not realize you were awake," George whispered in return.

"I am only just awake," Caesar said with a yawn, stretching against George's back.

The movement was erotic in the extreme and emphasized that both of them were naked and still a bit of a mess from the night before. It fascinated and terrified George in equal measure to be so comfortable in such a state.

As Caesar finished stretching, he slipped his arm back around George and tugged him flush against his chest. "I must admit to being surprised you're still here," he purred against George's ear, stroking a hand up his belly to his chest and toying with one of his nipples.

The rush of pleasure left George breathless and aching. He knew it was only a matter of time before Caesar reached between his legs to discover how hard his cock was.

"I am your prisoner," he told Caesar in return. "I cannot leave."

Caesar chuckled lazily, then planted a series of kisses over George's neck. "You are mine, that much is indisputable."

As if to prove his claim, he brushed his hand down George's body, leaving a trail of what felt like starlight in his wake. Instead of going straight for George's prick, he continued on to stroke his thigh, then lifted George's leg so that he could brace his own thigh between George's. The result was that George felt even more open and exposed.

That was when Caesar cupped his balls and played with them gently, sending waves of arousal through George.

"I must resist," George whispered, feeling as though he were losing the battle.

Caesar laughed softly and held George's balls tighter. "No, you must not. You must stop resisting what you so clearly desire."

"But—" George couldn't think of a single argument that made sense to him anymore, particularly when Caesar wrapped a hand around his cock and began to work him gently.

He let out an obscene moan and grabbed at Caesar's hand. Instead of pushing him away, though, he twined his fingers with Caesar's and joined him in stroking his cock. The pleasure of that simple gesture was beyond anything he thought was reasonable.

"That's it, darling," Caesar murmured against his ear, his own voice rich with arousal. "Come for me. Render unto Caesar the things that are Caesar's."

George caught his breath at the sacrilege of that statement...even as his body strained to do exactly as he'd been ordered to do. Caesar left his hand to lavish the head of George's cock with attention, pulling back his foreskin and teasing his fingertips against his slit to gather the moisture that had formed there. He used that to stroke George with more intensity, until George was a sighing, straining mass of pleasure in the man's arms.

With embarrassing speed, his orgasm raced through him, spilling his seed across Caesar's hand and the bedsheets. It felt so good that George thought he might lose his mind. The pleasure was so intense, and it was made beautiful by the care and tenderness of Caesar's caresses and the strain of the man's body against George's.

And then Caesar shocked him by raising his sticky fingers to his lips and thrusting them deep into his mouth to suck George's essence off them. The gesture should not have been as erotic as George found it to be.

"Ambrosia," Caesar purred, nuzzling against George's neck as his hand swept down, as if it would gather more. He touched George's oversensitive cock once more and asked, "Is this not Paradise?"

George let out a vocal breath that didn't form into words. Everything within him wanted to answer that yes, it was. He had never known pleasure like that was possible in the arms of another man. Caesar had opened his mind and his body to things he had not even dreamed of. He felt as though he'd only just begun to explore the mysteries of what his body was capable of.

But it was more than that. It was the soft bed and the nourishing food as well. It was the tenderness with which Caesar touched him, the sweetness of his kisses. Caesar wasn't merely a wicked taskmaster who demanded tribute in the form of bodily fluids. He had smiled at George and spoken kindly to him. They hadn't just tumbled through the evening and the night before, they'd conversed as well. They'd conversed as equals, as...as friends.

As it happened, Caesar had been watching him since he'd first begun to preach outside of Perdition, and he'd longed to learn more about him from the start. If George was honest, he'd noticed Caesar long before yesterday and wondered what sort of thoughts the man had as well.

George finally gathered the presence of mind to roll to his back so that he could gaze up into Caesar's beautiful face. He writhed with uncertainty, but it felt only right to ask, "Do you want me to...are you ready to...it seems only fair that I...."

Caesar laughed, then bent down to capture George's mouth in a kiss. They were both less than fresh, but somehow George didn't mind.

"You are a treasure," Caesar said as he lifted himself so

that he could stroke George's face while studying him. "One could argue that I have taken terrible advantage of you, and yet here you are, offering to bring me off as well."

"It...it seems only fair," George whispered.

Caesar's eyes sparkled with...affection? Is that what the Devil felt for his playthings?

"Yes, I am aroused," Caesar said, rubbing his erection against George's side to show as much. "But I can wait."

"For what?" George whispered, blinking up at him. He couldn't account for the tightness in his chest or the cozy sensations that pulsed through him.

"Forever," Caesar whispered, then bent down to kiss George again.

It was a beautiful, sensual kiss—one George could have enjoyed for hours. Could have, but a knock at the door startled them both instead.

"I asked not to be disturbed," Caesar cried out to the door, irritation marring his beautiful face.

"Your mother has sent word that she needs you right away," the deep voice of one of Perdition's other owners came through from the hall. "Some sort of trouble with a man named Roger?"

Caesar sighed heavily and sagged over George. George was utterly baffled by the whole thing, but reached up to stroke Caesar's side, as though he might provide some sort of comfort.

That caused Caesar to lift his head and smile at George.

"I'll be right there," Caesar called to the door, then pushed himself back until he knelt beside George. The movement caused the bedcovers to fall away, exposing both of their nakedness. "It seems we are needed elsewhere."

"Needed?" George asked, muscling himself up until he balanced on his elbows. He glanced down at his sweaty and seed-soiled body, then gazed with bated breath at Caesar's erection as it stood proudly between his legs. He feared he would lose his breath entirely at such a gorgeous sight, so he forced his eyes up to meet Caesar's and asked, "We?"

"Yes, of course, darling," Caesar said. He leaned forward and kissed George's mouth quickly before scrambling off the bed. "I'm taking you with me today. I have a feeling you will quite enjoy what I have to show you."

What he was showing George as he walked over to the washstand and poured water from the pitcher into the basin was his marvelous arse. George was overcome by the sudden urge to caress and to kiss it. And to bury his prick in it once again. The touch of redness between his cheeks from the times he'd done that the night before threatened to engorge George's cock all over again.

He threw off the bedcovers all the way and crawled out of bed, knowing that way lay madness. It was apparent that Caesar had business elsewhere that morning, and that it was important. He forced his thoughts out of bed along with the rest of him and joined Caesar at the washbasin.

"Your mother needs your help?" he asked as Caesar handed him a wet washcloth to clean away the evidence of the night they'd just spent together. "Is she the same woman as Constance?"

"No," Caesar answered with a laugh. "Though Mama would be flattered to hear you say that. They live on the same street, in the same building, though, and both of them look out for the residents there."

"And this Roger person?" George asked, washing as thoroughly as he could. It felt odd to wash in front of another man, particularly as that man had been the one to soil him in the first place.

Caesar's brow darkened into a scowl. "Roger is a blackguard, a drunk, and a wife-beater who I warned only yesterday to leave London or face the consequences."

George paused in the middle of scrubbing under his arms and gaped at Caesar. "And he is causing trouble again?"

"Apparently so," Caesar said, finishing with his own bath and heading to his wardrobe.

"What consequences will he face?" George asked, hurrying to catch up.

Caesar glanced over his shoulder at George as he opened the wardrobe. He grinned slyly and said, "Me."

A shiver shot down George's spine, but it was more than fear. Much more. He shouldn't have found Caesar's threats of violence so alluring. He shouldn't have found the Devil to be so attractive, one way or another. And he most certainly should not have wished to stay close to the man's side, no matter what sort of trouble he might lead George into.

They dressed and shaved as quickly as they could, then George was treated to another shock when Caesar walked right up to his bedchamber door and opened it without undoing a single lock.

"Has the door truly been unlocked this entire time?" George asked in a slightly strangled voice.

Caesar grinned at him and grasped his hand to lead him out of the room. "You could have left me whenever you wanted and no one, least of all me, would have stopped you."

It was a humbling confirmation of what he had suspected the day before—one that made George burn with guilt and hope and longing. He could have fled Perdition whenever he wanted to, but he hadn't even tried. He'd given in to temptation and stayed in the heart of sin...and even as he and Caesar passed through the house and out to the mews behind to mount horses that had been prepared for them, he couldn't find it within him to feel the sort of guilt he supposed he should feel.

He could have taken the horse Caesar offered him and rode away, back to his father and his righteous existence. He could have dashed straight to Bow Street to inform the runners of Perdition's illegal activities and have the place shut down. He could have taken himself straight to the nearest church and fallen to his knees to scourge himself for his sins.

Instead, he followed where Caesar led, through the finer streets of the city and on to less fortunate neighborhoods. All around him, he saw signs of poverty and privation. He saw people who needed help—filthy children, crippled men and women, even simply those who appeared to be sleeping off too much drink from the night before. He saw them...and in his mind, he heard his father's voice telling them all off as wastrels and degenerates.

Caesar clearly saw something different when he gazed upon them.

"What are you doing out so early, Moll?" he asked one woman who couldn't have been twenty yet, but who was hurrying along the street as though her house were on fire.

"Mama took a turn last night," Moll called back to him, as if she knew precisely who Caesar was...and respected him. "I've been to fetch the physician, but he refuses to come."

Caesar looked downright mutinous at that. "I'll make certain someone comes along directly. Do you have medicines for your mother?"

Moll looked forlorn. "We ran out, sir," she said.

Caesar reached into his pocket and pulled out a large

coin. He tossed it to Moll. "Fetch what she needs before you go home."

Moll's face lit up. "Thank you, sir, thank you!"

She changed directions, likely to seek out an apothecary's shop before going home.

George watched the exchange in awe. A maelstrom of feelings unsettled him.

Those feelings only intensified as they reached a street where quite a few people were already up and about, though the center of activity seemed to be around one particular man who was raging and struggling against two others who held him. An older woman stood at the top of a set of stairs leading to the doors of one of the buildings, and when she spotted Caesar approaching, her worried face broke into a smile of relief.

"Caesar!" she called out, waving. "Come quickly."

George immediately saw the resemblance between the older woman and Caesar. She must have been his mother. The crowd at the foot of the stairs went still at the sound of Caesar's name. Not only that, they parted so that Caesar and George could ride right into the thick of things.

"I warned you, Roger," Caesar said without preamble, glaring at the burly, half-drunk man being held by two others. "I told you to leave and never to come back."

"I got a right to me own wife," Roger slurred.

Caesar looked around. George looked as well, no idea what he was looking for.

"Where is Nancy?" Caesar asked.

"She's inside with the little ones," another woman said.

"They won't let me see my own children," Roger growled.

"Any man who beats his wife and gives his five-year-old son a black eye has forfeited his right to call himself a father," Caesar said from atop his horse. He seemed to address everyone, not just Roger. "I told you that if you ever came back, you would regret it." He gestured to the two men holding him, then said, "See to it Roger regrets it."

George's eyes went wide, even more so when the two men—both of whom were older and looked tougher than Caesar—nodded and dragged Roger away. Roger bellowed and struggled as he was taken off, but it was clear he was powerless to prevent his fate.

"They're not—" George began, then swallowed. "They're not going to kill the man, are they?"

Caesar grinned. "Probably not," he said in a way that was not at all reassuring. "They'll probably toss him in the Thames. Whether he can fish himself out or not is Roger's problem."

George wasn't certain whether he approved or not. Perhaps a man who beat his children deserved to be thrown in the Thames.

A moment later, all breath left George's lungs. How many times had his father beaten him, all in the name of the Lord? A rush of anger hit him. The Bible said to honor thy father and mother, but for the first time, George felt as though a bit of qualification was needed. Or, as Caesar had just said, any man who beat his children forfeited the right to call himself a father.

"Oy, Timothy," Caesar called out to one of the young men who was wandering away as Roger was taken off. "Go fetch Dr. Linley and take him to Moll's house. Her mother has taken a turn for the worse." He reached into his pocket, then tossed a coin to the young man. "Give him that to put some speed into him."

"Yes, sir," the man, Timothy called back then set off at a jog.

"Come along, George," Caesar said, back to smiling brightly as he dismounted. "Come down and meet my mother, and Constance. I was going to bring you here to help with today's activities regardless, but now you can gain firsthand experience with the sort of devil I am."

George opened his mouth, but nothing came out. He had no idea what Caesar meant. After an awkward pause, he swung his leg over and dismounted. A boy came forward to mind both the horses as George walked to Caesar's side. The only way to discover the depths of Caesar's devilry was to watch the man at work.

Chapter Six

I t was all a game. Everything about Caesar's life was a game—from Perdition, to the way he had charmed himself into his father's life, to the position he held in his old neighborhood, to the means by which he had thoroughly seduced George Mulgrew. But just because his life was a game, it didn't mean he failed to take it seriously, or that the stakes for himself and others weren't high.

He sent a fleeting glance to George to make certain he was not overwhelmed as he climbed the stairs to where his mother stood.

"Mama, you are looking well this morning," he said, folding her in his arms and pecking her cheek. "So well that I wonder whether I needed to be awoken so early this morning and dragged halfway across London to resolve a problem Davy and Norman seemed quite capable of resolving on their own." He arched an eyebrow at his mother.

His mother laughed and swatted his arm. "Do I need such an excuse to call for my own son?" she asked, smiling at him as though he had hung the stars.

"No," Caesar answered, grinning at her. "But do not be surprised if I come pounding on your door in the middle of the night, rousing you from a sound sleep, simply because I miss you." He bussed her cheek again, then stepped away, turning toward George.

Before he could make any introductions, his mother sent him a sideways look of knowing and murmured, "Sound sleep indeed. He still has the flush of passion in his cheeks."

Caesar laughed. "If you think those cheeks are red, you should see mine," he muttered back.

George overheard the exchange and began coughing for no reason, his eyes wide. Caesar couldn't hide his grin or his fondness as he shifted to George's side and slapped his back. He had always been completely open with his mother. His mother was no fainting violet either. And George was not the first person to be floored by the overly honest way the two of them spoke to each other. As far as Caesar was concerned, though, his mother's bawdy side was an example of the adage that the apple did not fall far from the tree.

Which filled Caesar with an even greater sense of giddiness as he hooked an arm around George's waist, turned to his mother, and said, "Mama, I would like you to meet Rev. George Mulgrew, saver of souls, redeemer of sinners, and very possibly the best man I have ever known." He added a hint of emphasis on the last word, giving it a Biblical connotation.

George nearly burst into another fit of coughing. He gaped at Caesar in disbelief for a moment, then cleared his throat, tugged on the bottom of his borrowed jacket, and faced Caesar's mother to say, "How do you do, ma'am," with a graceful bow.

That bow did something to Caesar's heart. His mother

echoed the sentiment ricocheting through him by placing her hands on her heart and gazing at George as though he were precious. Caesar could count on one hand the number of men who had shown his mother the sort of respect George was showing her. The sentiment of it went straight to Caesar's balls.

"George," Caesar continued the introduction, deliberately and scandalously addressing George by his given name, "this is my mother, Mrs. Betsy Potts."

Caesar's mother made a scoffing sound and waved her hand as if to dismiss the way Caesar had introduced her. "You can call me Mother Potts, like everyone else on this street and beyond does," she told George.

"Thank y—"

George barely got a word in before Caesar's mother stepped over to clasp him in her arms, hugging him so tightly that George's eyes bulged. Again, the sight was so sweet and precious that Caesar's chest squeezed. If things continued in that vein, he would become seriously worried that he had a heart ailment.

"Enough of these silly introductions," Constance interrupted, stepping up to join them. She smiled briefly at George, then turned to Caesar. "Now that you're here, you can assist us in feeding this rabble before the men scurry off to work. Most of them should already be on their way by now." She stared with particular ferocity at a young man who was likely no older than Caesar and George, but who looked worn and weathered in spite of his youth.

"George, this is Constance," Caesar introduced his friends much less formally than his mother. "She is the battleax who fancies herself even more of a mother to the poor unfortunates of this part of London than my mother."

George continued to look nonplussed at the scene

unfolding around him, but he managed another short bow and a, "How do you do?"

"I am overworked and scattered, sir, that is how I do," Constance said. She turned to Caesar. "Are you here to join us or to organize a country house party?"

"Here to join, of course," Caesar said, then turned to George. "Are we not?"

George blinked once, then seemed to come out of the stupor of surprise he'd found himself in. "Yes, we are here to help," he said.

A new sort of light flashed in George's brown eyes. It was different from the smoldering passion Caesar had seen there the night before and early that morning. It was much different from the desperate, zealous fire and stress that had radiated from the man for the past several months, as he'd gone about what he'd thought was his duty on Perdition's doorstep. It was a light that Caesar rather fancied and wanted to see more of.

"Where can I be of assistance?" George asked, glancing from Caesar to Constance to Caesar's mother.

"Nancy isn't just inside minding her babes," Constance said, taking charge. "She and Flora have been in there since well before dawn, making up porridge and baking with the supplies you sent down yesterday." She sent Caesar a fleeting look.

Caesar nodded in return. "I'm glad they were well-received. Where would you like to distribute these alms?" He peeked sideways to see what George thought.

They all set into motion, heading into the house to collect the food.

"I'd thought to set up a place in here where those who need it can be served," Constance said, "but there are people along the street who cannot get out to receive it, and those in the alleys who will not come here. You'll have to bring them whatever you can."

Caesar liked the sound of that. He would much rather spend his time walking through the streets and alleys of his old haunts, ensuring that all was well, the buildings were in good repair, and the people were not using the area he protected for activities that would bring harm to the men and women who fought to create better lives for themselves.

George seemed intent to do whatever Caesar wanted him to—which carried with it implications he would save for a time when they were alone. The eagerness with which George packed several baskets with bread and wedges of cheese and the enthusiasm with which he carried them out into the streets by Caesar's side was endearing.

"Do you do this often?" George asked half an hour later, after they'd delivered nourishment to a pair of elderly sisters who lived in the house across from Nancy's, and a young, exhausted mother with six young children who had been up through the night sewing in order to bring in the money she needed to feed her brood.

"What, wander the streets of East London, exposing myself to disease, danger, and worst of all, gossip?" Caesar asked with a teasing wink.

George's expression flattened as though he didn't appreciate Caesar's jest—which was an extremely heartening sign, as it meant the man was gaining comfort with him.

"No, I mean, do you distribute food to these people, give them money for medicines, and chase away indigent husbands on a frequent basis?" George asked.

Caesar thought about teasing his sweet curate a bit more as they headed down a particularly fetid alley, pausing to give a small loaf of bread and a bit of cheese to an old man who was missing one leg. There was a time for teasing and there was a time for the truth, though, and he and George had reached a moment of truth.

"Yes, in fact, I do," he said. He rested his hand comfortingly on the old man's head for a moment, heedless of whatever lice or sores the man might have, then walked on to where he spotted another lost soul in the alley's shadows.

George didn't seem to have anything to say—though his eyes said quite a bit on their own, all of it encouraging—so Caesar continued.

"Perdition is vastly profitable. In addition to that, I have an allowance from my father, even though I am his bastard and not one of his brood. I have everything I could possibly desire within the walls of the club, and I do not have the constitution for hoarding or letting abundance turn me into a spendthrift, as some men do."

He paused again so that they could give more of their food to a young woman who was weeping, huddled in the shadows. George seemed particularly moved by the woman's plight, and when Caesar moved on, George crouched beside the woman and began speaking softly to her, too quiet for Caesar to hear.

Caesar backed off a few steps and watched silently as George clasped the woman's tiny hands in his and continued to speak to her. Whatever he said, the woman glanced to him with wide, hopeful eyes and stopped weeping. George stroked a hand over her head, which seemed to prompt the woman to speak in quick, tense tones, also too quiet for Caesar to hear.

Caesar felt more and more as though he were intruding, so he backed farther toward the end of the alley, continuing to watch. George took the bread from the woman's hands, said something while using it as a way to emphasize his point, then handed it back to her and wrapped her hands around it. Then, if Caesar could believe his eyes, it seemed as though the two of them fell into some sort of prayer together.

Caesar's heart pounded against his ribs, particularly when George laid his hands on the woman's head as if he were blessing her. He was so affected that tears threatened. He'd never been in the presence of something holy before, but George made him feel that way. Not just as he ministered to the young woman, but when they had been together before. His mind and heart filled with the memory of the two of them in the throes of passion, but it somehow mingled with what he witnessed now, forming a rush of powerful emotion that touched every part of him, from his heart to his cock and beyond.

"Sorry," George said once he'd left the woman and resumed walking with Caesar. "She was clearly in need of succor, and I felt called to ease her distress."

"No, no, it's fine," Caesar said, his voice hoarse with emotion. He blinked rapidly to clear his thoughts and feelings as they stepped out onto the next street. "It was quite beautiful, actually."

"Truly?" George stared at him in surprise.

Caesar was just as surprised. "Did you not find it beautiful?"

George opened his mouth, but no sound came out at first. "Yes, of course," he said at last. "But I would have thought a hardened devil like you would find such ministrations to be trite and useless."

A flash of indignation hit Caesar before he caught the glint in George's eyes. The bastard was teasing him—teasing him in the way Caesar usually teased.

Caesar's heart felt as though it might fill to bursting in his chest. If he could have, he would have thrown the basket of bread aside, grabbed George by his face, slammed him into the nearest wall, and kissed the man until they were both panting puddles of arousal.

He was stopped from doing so as a young girl raced up to him and grabbed the bottom of his jacket.

"If you please, Mr. Potts, sir," she said, staring up at him with wide, round eyes. "Mama is poorly. The baby's coming. She asked me to fetch the surgeon, but I don't know where he is."

Caesar's thoughts were wrenched away from his need to ravish George. "Lead the way," he told the girl, sparing a brief glance to George to make certain he was coming.

The woman in question was on the second floor of a building only a few doors down. As they entered, Caesar handed his basket off to an adolescent girl loitering on the front steps, telling her to take it to Constance one street over and to inform her and his mother of the situation.

Once that was done, Caesar and George rushed upstairs to find the laboring mother.

"Mr. Potts," the woman gasped and panted at the sight of him. She was on her feet, pacing the cramped, single room she and her daughter, and, it seemed, a toddler who cried on the floor in the corner, lived in. "Lordy, what are you doing here? I sent Pru to fetch the surgeon."

"Help is on the way," Caesar told the woman, unbuttoning his jacket and shrugging out of it. "In the meantime, we are here to assist in any way we can."

The woman answered with a painful moan as she was hit with another contraction. Caesar leapt straight into action, sliding an arm around the woman and walking with her back to the bed. He knew next to nothing about bringing babies into the world, but it was a weak man who panicked in the face of the unknown when someone desperately needed help.

As Caesar rubbed the woman's back and helped her through her pain, George removed his jacket and rolled up his sleeves as well. He checked to make certain the kettle steaming on the stove had enough water, then, to Caesar's surprise, crossed the room to lift the wailing toddler into his arms to comfort the child.

Again, his heart and soul throbbed and ached at the sight of George with the child. The boy—at least, Caesar thought it was a boy, though it was hard to tell with the shapeless garment the child wore—settled almost at once, clinging to George. Once that was in hand, George joined Caesar with the laboring mother, both of them soothing her and helping her.

Twenty minutes later, the door burst open and an older woman who Caesar knew to be Mrs. Harris, the midwife, strode into the room.

"There, there, now," Mrs. Harris said, marching right over to the laboring mother. "All is well. Tell me how your labor is progressing."

Before the woman could give her more than the most basic information, Mrs. Harris turned to Caesar and George and said, "This is no place for men. Take the babies down to Alice and let her mind them."

"Yes, Mrs. Harris," Caesar said with a cheeky degree of deference for the woman.

Mrs. Harris sent him a sly grin in return, but there was no time for more banter. Caesar and George made a quick exit as the laboring mother moaned with another contraction.

Once they were back on the street and had handed care

of both the toddler and little Pru over to the adolescent girl, Alice, Caesar and George burst into laughter.

"That was not what I expected at all," Caesar said, retrieving his basket of food, glancing around to assess where they were and where they needed to go, then grinning at George.

George's entire countenance was alive with excitement. "I take it that does not happen often?"

"Hardly at all," Caesar laughed, slapping a hand on George's shoulder. He grew a bit more serious as he said, "I am generally witness to the other end of life, I'm afraid. But in truth, it brings me joy whenever I hear of a new soul being born into this world. I do not care one whit how the babe got here, whether through a godly union of righteous people or as the whelp of a street whore with no idea who the father might be. Life is precious, and any life brought into this world should be given a chance to become something glorious."

George's smile had faded through Caesar's sentimental speech. He slowed his steps when Caesar stopped speaking and simply stood where he was, staring at him. Caesar paused and turned back to him, attempting to interpret the strange, new look that George wore. It wasn't anger or disapproval. It wasn't sadness or melancholy either. It might have been akin to despair...or perhaps adoration.

"I...." George snapped his mouth closed and continued to gaze at Caesar with a puzzled frown for a few more seconds before trying again. "You care about these people," he said at last. "You truly care about them. Not just for show or...or out of some sense of duty."

"Of course, I do," Caesar said with a soft smile. "They are my friends and were my neighbors. I have watched their triumphs and their failures from the time I was a boy."

George took a step closer to him. "But you honestly care about them, even though they can do nothing for you."

Caesar laughed, though the intensity in George's eyes and the storm of emotions he could see George was experiencing unnerved him. "I like people," he said with a shrug. "I like them as they are. Every person has their ways and their stories. They might not be the right ways or the stories your sort like to hear, but they are unique and amazing."

Caesar worried he'd skated too close to accusing George of something when his sweetheart's face pinched into misery. He took a step forward, feeling the need to comfort George, but George held up a hand to stop him.

"This is God's work," he said staring down at nothing, as though realizing something that could shatter the earth. "This is what it means to feed His flock and to tend His sheep. This is what we have been charged to do from the very start." He pulled his gaze up to meet Caesar's. "To love one another as He has loved us."

Caesar smiled gently, stepping closer to George than he should have in public view. He took a bit of a risk and rested his free hand on the side of George's face. "I have never thought of it in that way before," he confessed. He'd rarely given God's words much thought, he'd merely done what he was moved to do.

The temptation to act on his feelings in yet another way was too great for him to ignore. Even if they were observed, Caesar had enough power on that particular street to have his actions go unnoticed by anyone who might object.

He leaned in and kissed George's lips tenderly. "What a horrible, unrepentant sinner you have found yourself captured by, eh?"

He kissed George again, brushed his thumb over the man's hot cheek, then stepped away, continuing on with their errand as though his place in the world hadn't just suddenly made itself known to him.

"Come along, darling," he said, reaching his hand back to George as a gesture for his sweetheart to follow. "We have more of the Devil's work to do before we go on to our great reward."

Chapter Seven

A thousand conflicting thoughts and emotions passed through George's mind and heart as the morning wore on and he and Caesar continued with their mission to feed and tend to the poor. So much needed to be done, from distributing food that Caesar had paid for to visiting the elderly and infirm to determine whether they needed more care than two young men could give them.

Caesar was extraordinarily free with his money—of which he'd brought quite a bit with him—and his touch. George didn't think much of it at first, but after witnessing his captor holding gnarled hands while listening to older men and women who probably rarely received calls, embracing children who appeared in dire need of affection, and kissing the cheeks of several downtrodden mothers who were too exhausted to do more than smile in thanks, George could see that touch was as precious an offering as coins.

His own father would rather have died than touch any of the beggars he preached to on streetcorners, or even the wealthy members of the aristocracy whom he was always chasing after for patronage. George couldn't imagine the man fetching a handkerchief to hold for the ill to cough into or allowing a colicky baby to spit up on his shoulder. In fact, George couldn't imagine his father doing even the meanest of tasks that he and Caesar dove into with vigor throughout the morning.

"You seem subdued," Caesar commented as the two of them waited on the doorstep of that first house, where Nancy and Caesar's mother lived, as their horses were fetched to take them back to St. James's. When George glanced distractedly at him, Caesar grinned and said, "Have I unsettled you?"

George opened his mouth to reply, but thought about his words instead. Yes, Caesar had most definitely unsettled him. In so many ways that George had lost count.

Instead of admitting as much, he said, "My father has always expounded on the necessity of living a Christian life, of humbling oneself before God and viewing oneself as a vice-ridden worm in need of repentance. His entire theology is built around exhorting sinners to repent and live a holy life so that they might be rewarded by Paradise."

He paused, knowing in his heart how to finish his thoughts, but the words wouldn't pass his lips for some reason.

Caesar said nothing. The gorgeous, infuriating, paradoxical man merely grinned at him with a knowing flash in his eyes. He knew precisely what George was thinking, which came as a surprise relief. George wouldn't have to admit to the deep, painful thought that had been tearing his heart in twain through the entire morning.

He had been wrong. He had been so very wrong. Not only about Caesar, but about what it meant to lead a good life and to do God's work. The truth upended his entire world.

"Come along," Caesar said, his grin turning sympathetic as he pushed away from the wall where he'd been leaning. "The boys are here with the horses. A nice ride through the city will clear your head of these meddlesome thoughts."

He winked as he passed George, taking his hand and leading him down to the street.

George let out a heavy breath and received his mount from the boy who had brought the horse from the mews. He noted that Caesar paid the two boys a generous amount as he mounted, then waited for Caesar to lead the way.

They rode back to Perdition in relative silence. One or two neighbors from Caesar's streets called out thanks and blessings to them before they reached the end of the street, and Caesar responded merrily, promising he would return. George believed he would return. He had witnessed Caesar at work—perhaps his true work—and he felt certain Caesar would not abandon the people who relied on him.

The world they left behind was a far cry from the fine and comfortable world they rode into on the way to Perdition. It was such a contrast that George saw the neatly-kept gardens and well-dressed pedestrians strolling the streets with new eyes. How many of the men and women that they passed in their silks and lace even knew of the people like Constance, or even little Pru, or the desperate young prostitute he'd prayed with in the alley? How many of them would lift a finger to help where help was needed? And yet, Caesar helped them.

"Here we are," Caesar announced as they rode into the mews behind Perdition. "My humble slice of Hell." He grinned as though everything were fine with the world as he dismounted, then gestured for George to do the same.

George climbed down from his horse and handed it over to the stable boy that rushed forward to take it. When Caesar gestured for him to follow him into the club, George went without question.

Perdition was bustling with activity as they entered. At least, the downstairs area was.

"Sir, the greengrocer has made his delivery, and I don't think you'll like it," a grey-haired matron who looked as though she could snap George in two told Caesar as they passed the kitchen.

Caesar paused and turned back to the woman. "Why, Mrs. Fuller? What seems to be the matter with it?" he asked.

Mrs. Fuller frowned and planted her fists on her ample hips. "Half of it is wilted, the other half not yet fully grown." Her scowl deepened, and she went on with, "If I've told him once I've told him a dozen times, it don't matter who he's selling his produce to, if it's not of the best quality, he'll be sorry once you hear about it."

George was startled by that threat, but Caesar merely laughed at it. "I shall have a word with him as soon as I can. Likely tomorrow. Can you use what he's brought in the meantime?"

"I can, sir," Mrs. Fuller sighed.

"Good." Caesar nodded. "We shall make do." He continued on, George following, but turned back to say, "Oh, Mrs. Fuller, could you have luncheon sent up to my room? Rev. Mulgrew and I have yet to eat. Luncheon, that is." He winked.

Mrs. Fuller sent George a cheeky smile that had George's face burning. "Right away, sir."

Caesar laughed, and he and George continued on, up

the stairs and through the servants' door into the main hallway of Perdition.

"Mrs. Fuller is the best housekeeper in London," he explained as they strode on past what appeared to be an office where one of Caesar's partners was working, past a small parlor where some sort of intense card game was taking place, and past another room that was filled with giddy laughter. "She used to run a brothel in Spitalfields, but says she's much happier ordering us all about in Perdition."

George didn't know what to think. Mrs. Fuller hadn't seemed like a wicked woman. Stern and unbending, yes, but not...well, not what he had been led to believe whores were like. Then again, his entire perception of the order of sinners and saints had been crushed into a confusing pile of dust around his feet.

"Oh, Mr. Potts, sir."

They were stopped again as a young woman wearing not much at all dashed out of the room filled with laughing people. She was plump and rosy, and her state of undress only served to show that she was in the peak of good health.

Caesar paused at the foot of the stairs to turn and smile at her. "Yes, Hattie?"

George stepped back as the woman, Hattie, scurried right up to Caesar. "If you please, sir," she said with a look of adoration for Caesar, "it's my sister's birthday next week. Mama would like us all to have supper together to mark the occasion. Might I have the night off?"

George's brow shot up. It felt unheard of for a whore employed at a gaming hell to request a night off for something as banal as a sister's birthday supper.

But Caesar smiled, rested a hand on the woman's cheek,

and said, "Of course, love. I'll send along a little trinket for your sister as well."

"Thank you, sir," Hattie said, clutching her hands to her heart and bobbing a quick curtsy before turning and dashing back into the room of giggling people.

Caesar chuckled and shook his head, then he and George continued up the stairs.

George's head spun. He could not believe that a mere twenty-four hours before, he had stood on the doorstep of Perdition, railing against the many sins that the house contained and warning men to stay away, lest they lose their immortal souls.

Now, as he followed Caesar down the hall, then into his bedchamber, his opinions on the matter had been reversed.

"Come on," Caesar said with a teasing grin, stepping so close to George that George could smell the faded notes of that morning's soap and the honest scent of Caesar's skin. "Tell me what has put that lost look on your handsome face." Before George could do more than turn his head to Caesar, Caesar added, "I already know what it is, mind you, but I want to hear the words from you."

George let out a breath, his shoulders dropping. "If you already know, then why do you require me to say the words?"

Caesar laughed. "Because I am the Devil and your captor, or do you not remember? It is my solemn duty to torture you and to make you do things against your will. Though I might add, one thing I did not need to force or torture you into doing is returning to my bedchamber."

He inched even closer, sliding an arm around George's waist and holding George's chin so that he could sweep his thumb across George's lips. The action had George instantly breathless.

"You could have run at any moment," Caesar told him in a soft, seductive voice. "You could have fled from the streets we walked, taken my horse and flown off, or refused to enter this room again with me. Yet, here you are."

Even with the turmoil and confusion that gripped him, some things felt so clear to George as the heat of Caesar's body infused him that it was as though the voice of Truth had spoken to him directly.

"I am here because this is where I want to be," he said in an almost reverent hush. "What I witnessed today is what I have spent my entire life yearning for."

"And what is that, love?" Caesar asked, stroking the side of his face and staring with amorous intent at George's lips.

"Kindness," George said. "True charity. Serving the poor and lifting up those who cannot lift themselves."

His heart raced with the speed and intensity of the realizations that enveloped him. He clung to Caesar, tracing a hand over the man's strong jaw and gazing into his smiling eyes.

"I took up the cloth because I felt called to help people," he said. "It is all I have ever wanted. My father took it upon himself to form and instruct me, but his way is not God's way at all. It feels mad to say it to the Devil, but your way is the way I want."

Caesar smiled. "I have no objections to you striving to do things my way," he said.

George wasn't prepared for it, but when Caesar surged into him, slanting his mouth over his and kissing him in a way that seemed to steal all the breath from his lungs, he gave in to it. Not just gave in, he relished it. He was a complete novice at kissing—at affection and arousal and love in general—but he promised himself he would be a quick learner, and he kissed Caesar back with everything he had.

Which was why he jerked so hard in Caesar's arms when a knock sounded at the door, followed by a young voice saying, "Your luncheon, sir."

Caesar laughed. The sound stoked George's desire even more.

"Are you always being interrupted like this?" George asked through panting breaths.

"Unfortunately, yes," Caesar laughed again, letting go and stepping toward the door. "It is one of the perils of being the chief devil in Hell."

George's mouth twitched with mirth as Caesar answered the door and received a tray from Sarah. One day ago, he would not have found such a jest amusing at all. One day before, he would not have watched Caesar's every move with hungry eyes as he took the tray to the table. It floored George that the world could change so fast.

But perhaps it hadn't changed. Perhaps the feelings that pulsed through him now had been there all along, and he'd only just had the chains his father had bound him in broken so that his true self could be set free.

"Would you like to eat first or engage in craven acts of depravity instead?" Caesar asked with pretend casualness as he turned away from the table.

George didn't hesitate for a moment. "Craven acts of depravity, please," he said, hardly believing his own words.

"I was hoping you would say that," Caesar purred, already loosening his neckcloth as he stalked across the room to George.

A voice within George warned him that he was in danger, but it was so much quieter than it had ever been that it was easy to ignore. He started in on the buttons of his borrowed jacket and waistcoat as Caesar did the same, and by the time the two of them met, it was all they could do to breathe as they threw themselves at each other, kissing and caressing and tugging at each other's clothing.

George lost track of what he was doing and was only aware of peeling out of his clothes as it meant Caesar's hands and mouth could reach his bare skin. He groaned with arousal, spiraling out of control at an alarming rate, as Caesar rained soft kisses and sharper nips with his teeth across George's shoulders and the top of his chest. He reveled in the sensations, and he threaded his fingers though Caesar's soft hair, digging his fingers into the man's scalp as he moved his kisses lower.

"Yes, do that," Caesar gasped, taking the moment to toss aside his shirt and undo the fall of his breeches. "Pull my hair, grip me tightly enough to leave bruises. I love it."

George's mouth fell open in shock, but Caesar used that to crash into another kiss. The intensity of the passion he felt was so heady that George didn't second guess himself for a moment before kissing Caesar back and thrusting his tongue into the man's mouth.

The next few moments were a whirlwind of sensation and erotic sounds that issued from both of them as they removed the rest of their clothes and their boots. Somehow, George found himself perched on the very edge of Caesar's bed, his legs spread wide, with Caesar kneeling between them. George balanced himself with one hand while following Caesar's orders and gripping the man's hair tightly with his other. Caesar lavished George's chest and stomach with kisses and licks, then planted a few briefly on George's inner thighs before closing his mouth around one of George's balls.

George's eyes went wide, and he let out a surprised

moan as Caesar sucked gently. He'd never imagined such a thing were possible, let alone that it would be so pleasurable. That pleasure was doubled and more when Caesar licked his way up his hard, pulsing shaft, taking a moment to pull back his foreskin, then licking at the moisture that had formed on his cockhead like it was the sweetest nectar.

George's whole body began to shake with desire as Caesar played with him, and when Caesar drew his entire cockhead into his mouth, licking and sucking for a moment, before bearing down on him and taking him all the way to the back of his throat, until his face was buried in the wiry hair of George's groin, George let out a wild cry.

It was utter madness, but George couldn't get enough of it. He gripped Caesar's hair tighter and couldn't stop himself from jerking even deeper into the man's throat. Caesar choked—which produced a sensation that felt astoundingly good—but before he could even think to feel shame or remorse for his actions, Caesar made a sound of pure ecstasy. He encouraged George to choke him again, which he did, causing both of them to make wild sounds.

Caesar liked a bit of rough treatment. It was a revelation to George. Caesar was still the one in control, but George imagined himself as an instrument Caesar could wield to draw exactly what he wanted from him. The paradox of being used as a bludgeon of pleasure was too beautiful and too much for him to comprehend. Before he truly realized what was happening, his body flew out of control, and he spilled his seed in heady waves of pleasure down Caesar's throat.

Caesar made every sort of obscene sound George could think of as he moaned and sputtered and swallowed everything George could give him. When George lost his ability to hold himself up and flopped back against the bed, Caesar let his cock go with a slick sound and gasped for breath as he straightened. He leaned heavily against the bed, arching over George and balancing on one hand while reaching for one of George's hands.

He brought George's hand to his hard, hot cock and wrapped George's fist around him. He showed George what to do for a few strokes before removing his own hand and demanding, "Make me come."

George did exactly as ordered, unsurprised that Caesar was already so aroused it took only a few strokes. The sounds Caesar made were heavenly as the man balanced above him while George handled him to orgasm. George caught his breath as Caesar tensed and warm jets of seed spilled across his wrist and his belly. The contorted expression Caesar wore as he spilled himself went straight to George's heart. The Devil was beautiful when he was at his wickedest.

When it was done, they collapsed together onto the bed, writhing together, kissing between gasps for breath, and running their hands over each other's bodies—not so much for pleasure, but for reassurance. And reassurance was precisely what George needed. Because he knew where his heart lay now. He knew his true calling and the place where he could do the most good. He knew where he was meant to be, not only in that moment, but for all the moments to come. He was meant to be in Caesar's arms.

Chapter Eight

For the second morning in a row, Caesar awoke with George in his bed. Naked. Just the way he wanted the man. While George continued to slumber—truly, the poor thing needed the sleep after the activities Caesar had engaged him in the evening before, likely after the life he'd been living as well—Caesar propped himself on one arm and watched him with a smile.

George was beautiful in so many ways. He was artless, for one. He wore his convictions on his sleeves, even when those convictions were as changeable as the shifting sands. There was a definite charm to a man who was willing to let his uncertainty show, particularly when it distressed him.

And George had been distressed.

All through the day they had spent together, in the midst of serving the poor and unfortunate and in the two of them tangling together as Caesar schooled his darling curate in all the ways of passion, George had been unsettled. Caesar had caught the pinch of his brow or the purse of his lips when George hadn't thought he was watching. Caesar understood full well what his sweetheart was up against—

aside from being up against him. Everything that George had been taught to believe about the world and his place in it—and about Heaven and Hell—had been shown to be as hollow as a dried-up bone.

George stirred as sleep began to leave him, and Caesar's smile grew. Even the way George moved was honest and open. He rolled to his back and stretched, his closed eyes pinching as he likely felt the twinge of the muscles he'd used the evening before. Caesar stroked his fingertips across George's face, tracing the man's full, sensual lips with particular care. He could spend a lifetime kissing those lips and not grow tired of it.

Which was a ridiculous notion, really. George was but a moment in his life. A beautiful one, that much was certain, but temporary. How could he be more? Their lives were as different as chalk and cheese. George might profess to want to serve the poor now, but how would he feel when he saw more of the life Caesar lived, more of the gambling and wantonness of Perdition, and more of the trouble that sort of business brought with it?

George's eyes fluttered open, and when he smiled up at Caesar, letting out a breath of contentment, Caesar's heart lurched in his chest and his doubts seemed trivial.

"Good morning," he said, continuing to trace his fingertips around George's face, then down his neck to his chest.

"Good morning," George murmured in return. He shivered slightly as Caesar toyed with one of his nipples, then continued downward to caress George's morning wood.

"Did you sleep well, my angel?" Caesar asked, teasing George's cock into full wakefulness.

"I did," George replied with a sigh. "Perhaps better than I have in my life."

Caesar hummed fondly, smiling at the flush that came

to his sweetheart's face as he continued to stroke George's cock. "Do you know what makes for a glorious awakening of a morning?" he asked, the work of his hand picking up speed as he leaned closer to kiss the corner of George's mouth.

George's only response was to sigh and moan and to arch his hips into Caesar's touch.

There was something erotic and powerful in the way George surrendered his body entirely as Caesar stroked him to orgasm. Whatever inhibitions the good reverend had been hiding behind two days before, he had abandoned them completely. He was as wanton as any of the men Perdition paid to ply their trade with the customers downstairs as he whimpered and panted, then jerked his hips to urge things along right before tilting his head back and letting out a cry of bliss as his seed spilled over Caesar's hand. Caesar watched him for any signs of remorse, but there wasn't even a touch of guilt in his darling's expression as he settled into a sated half-sleep while catching his breath.

Caesar kissed George's cheek, then climbed over him and out of bed to begin his day. He could ignore his cock's demands for the time being. All that mattered was that George was sated. He would demand repayment from his sweetheart that evening, when the day's work was done.

And there was quite a bit of work awaiting him. Taking a day to provide for his old neighbors was important to him, but it generally made for a full slate of work at the club the next day.

Caesar had washed thoroughly and dressed before George stirred again. He had already lathered his face for a shave when George muscled himself to sit against the pillows, finally looking uncertain after the carnal confidence with which he'd awakened.

"I suppose you'll want me to go away now," he said, the most charming look of disappointment in his warm brown eyes.

Caesar raised his eyebrows as he dragged the razor over his face. "Whyever would I want that?" he asked, grinning.

George sent him a look that was ridiculously bashful, considering all they'd shared in the last two days. "I know I am not your prisoner," he said, picking at the bedclothes. "I know that I am free to go at any time. It is just...." He blew out a breath through his nose, then seemed to come to a decision.

He threw back the bedclothes and climbed out of bed. Instead of marching up to Caesar, he took himself to the washbasin to bathe. He picked up the cloth and soap as though he had a right to them, as though they were his own. Watching that sent a thrill of something close to lust through Caesar, but was a different emotion entirely, a deeper one. It was almost as though George belonged there, naked and bathing in Caesar's bedchamber.

"I've a great deal of work today," Caesar said as he finished shaving, figuring George needed a bit of help to get where he needed to be. George's shoulders sagged a bit, until Caesar continued on with, "I would welcome any sort of assistance you might give me, if clerical work and sorting accounts is something you feel competent to do."

George glanced up at Caesar across the washbasin, his entire countenance lighting. "Truly? You would...you would not mind if I...stayed?"

Caesar caught his breath. He couldn't remember the last time he'd heard more beautiful words. "If that is what you wish," he said.

Sunlight and joy seemed to infuse George. "Yes, that is what I wish."

Caesar smiled back at him. It was a genuine smile, not teasing or wicked or designed to overpower the good curate. It was an expression that came from a new place in his heart, one that made him feel younger than his years.

"Very well, then," he said, finishing with his razor and wiping his face. "You are welcome to whatever clothing of mine you would like, as well as whatever else you need to finish bathing and shaving."

George smiled at him in thanks, then got on with washing up and dressing. Caesar busied himself around the room, tidying things that didn't need tidying and biding his time, watching George and relishing the warm sensations inside himself. Perhaps it wasn't so ridiculous to entertain the idea of keeping George. After the way he'd thrown so much of himself into helping the poor, Caesar was certain he could find some sort of employment for him at the club.

Those thoughts sang in Caesar's heart as George finished dressing and shaving, then as the two of them made their way down to the ground floor. His mind was already hard at work coming up with arguments he could use with his partners to convince them to let George say. As much as Caesar would have liked to think he could do just as he pleased, he had an entire house full of other men and women to consider. Their safety was important.

Hard on the heels of those thoughts, before he and George had made it all the way down the grand staircase into the front hall, the slight disturbance Caesar had heard from a distance the moment they'd left his bedchamber burst into a full fracas.

"There he is!" a dour, middle-aged man with a sallow complexion called from just inside the door. Jasper and

Simon were working to hold the man back, but he pointed up the stairs, fury contorting his features, and shouted, "There is my son!"

Caesar felt George freeze beside him. He descended two more steps before realizing George wasn't coming. When he twisted to glance back at George, his sweetheart had lost all color.

"Father," George said in a strangled voice. "Wh-what are you doing here?"

The man by the door, the other Rev. Mulgrew, glared at George as though he were a demon. "What have they done to you?" he hissed. "What is this villainy I see before me?"

"I can explain," George said. He teetered slightly—so much so that Caesar reached out to him—then started heavily down the stairs.

"There is nothing to explain," Rev. Mulgrew growled, sending vengeful looks at Caesar, Jasper, and Simon. "I can see with my own eyes what has transpired here. You have snared my son in your wicked web and have corrupted him. You have turned him away from all that is good and holy and mired him in your sins."

Caesar followed as George approached his father. He couldn't exactly argue with the man. He had, in a way, done all of those things.

"Father, there has been a grave mistake," George said as he moved to stand in front of his father.

Caesar's heart went out to him. It was as clear as day to him that George was doing his very best to stand up to the man who had loomed over him from the time he was a child. It could not have been easy, not at all, and yet, George was trying. Caesar stepped up behind him, reaching to rest a hand of encouragement on George's back.

Before he could touch his darling, Rev. Mulgrew roared,

"You will not lay your filthy, cloven hoof on my son!" He grabbed George's arm and yanked him toward the front door. "We are leaving at once."

To his credit, George gave his father a look of utter indignation at the way he was being jerked about like a child. Paradoxically, George was the one who looked like a man, while his father demonstrated all the peevishness of a child whose toy had been taken from him.

"I do not wish to go, Father," George said, attempting to stand his ground.

His father whipped around and sneered at him. "Has the Devil wheedled his way so deeply into you?" he demanded.

Caesar forced himself not to snort with laughter. Quite the contrary, George had been the one deep, deep inside of him the night before, just the way he liked it.

"These are not wicked people, Father," George insisted. "There is more to this gaming hell than you could possibly imagine."

It helped nothing that as soon as George spoke, Hattie appeared at the top of the stairs wearing nothing but a banyan that was completely open in front, exposing her fully. She stopped on the top stair with a squeak, blinking at Rev. Mulgrew in confusion.

"Do we have custom so early?" she asked, then glanced over her shoulder at the hall she'd just come from. "I could tidy up my room and be ready in ten minutes."

"Harlot!" Rev. Mulgrew hissed. He grabbed George and yanked the man in front of him, as if he could shield himself from sin. Caesar noted the fire of lust in Rev. Mulgrew's eyes as he drank in the sight of Hattie, though. "Jezebel! Is this what has kept you out for days, boy?" he demanded of George. "Is this harlot the reason you have not returned to your true and godly home?"

Caesar's mouth twitched again, but George remained perfectly serious. "No, Father, this is not what has kept me in Perdition." His gaze flickered to Caesar.

"You lie!" Rev. Mulgrew shouted, then cuffed George on the side of his head. Caesar lost all of his mirth and lunged forward. But before he could say anything, Rev. Mulgrew went on with, "I will have the full force of the law brought down on this house of sin! I will go straight to the constable, straight to Bow Street! I will go to the king himself to have your wickedness exposed and every man and woman in this place thrown into gaol, or Bedlam!"

Caesar lost his humor over the situation again. "You will not," he growled.

"You will not," George echoed, resignation in his voice. He let out a breath and seemed to reach some sort of decision. He turned to his father and said, "I will come home with you, Father. And I will explain why there is no need to continue to rail against this place."

"There is always a need to defeat evil and crush sin beneath your heel," his father went on, angrier than ever. "They have corrupted your mind, boy. I will scourge the sin out of you and wash the Devil from your mind. Come!"

The order was cold and definitive. Everything within Caesar wanted to rush to defend his love. He had no doubt that George would face violence when he was in his father's house once again. But when he took a step forward, George raised a hand to ward him off.

"I will deal with this," George said quietly but firmly.

That simple statement made Caesar feel helpless, and if there was one thing he hated above all else, it was feeling helpless. All he could do was nod to George and force himself to trust that the man knew what he was doing.

No, there was more than that. As George ushered his father out through the front door—Rev. Mulgrew continuing to hurl insults and curses as he went—Caesar had to force himself to trust that George would come back to him.

As soon as the door slammed shut—Rev. Mulgrew's action, not George's or anyone's within the house—Caesar stood where he was, staring at the door, his heart beating in his throat and his hands numb with fear. He hadn't realized until that moment how much he wanted George, truly wanted him. Not as a plaything or a diversion, as a part of himself. He had never known a man as wonderful or as good as George.

And he had let the man walk out of his life. He'd let George go without truly telling the man how full his heart felt when George was around, or how much he made him smile, or how the pulse of arousal beat constantly within him when he was in George's presence. He hadn't congratulated George for a job well done the day before, not in words, at least. He hadn't told the man he loved him.

"Oh, dear," Simon said, striding up behind Caesar and clapping a hand on his shoulder. "I believe we have a problem."

"We most certainly do," Jasper said, walking over to join them.

Caesar shook his head to clear his thoughts, then headed toward the nearest parlor and the tray of spirits that every room in Perdition contained.

"We do not have a problem," he muttered as he poured himself a glass of whatever came to his hand first. "Rev. Mulgrew has no true power. I doubt he will follow through on his threat to go to the authorities. Even if he does, I doubt they would listen to him."

He was certain of none of that, though, and his hand shook as he raised the glass to his mouth.

Jasper and Simon had followed him into the room, chuckling.

"That's not the problem he means," Simon said.

Caesar whipped around to face him, spilling some of his drink as he did. "What do you mean?" he asked. "Do we have a greater concern? Did something happen while George and I were out yesterday?"

Jasper and Simon exchanged an amused look.

"'George and I,'" Jasper said, grinning as though he'd solved a clever riddle.

Simon laughed, then turned to Caesar. "Our boy here is in love," he said.

"Actual love," Jasper agreed. "Not like any of those fleeting dalliances he's had in the past."

"Certainly not," Simon agreed. "And he's in love with a man of the cloth, no less."

"I am not—" Caesar stopped himself before he told the greatest lie of his life. If George could be honest about his thoughts and emotions, then so could he.

He took a deep breath and set the half-finished tumbler of spirits back on the tray.

"Alright," he admitted, facing his partners again. "I will admit it. I am in love with George Mulgrew. But there isn't a damn thing I can do about it."

Jasper and Simon exchanged another amused look.

"I do not see that there is anything you must do about it," Jasper said. "You are in love. It's sweet."

"Should we prepare an extra room for young Rev.

Mulgrew upon his return?" Simon asked. "Or should we all just assume he will be sharing your room henceforth."

"I do not know that he will return," Caesar said, dreading the words as he spoke them. He marched forward, bumping Simon's shoulder as he headed back to the hall, then down toward the office. His friends followed, so he called back to them, "I do not know if George will ever return. Not if his father has his way."

"Oh, the lad will return, alright," Jasper laughed. "He wore the same love-bitten look that you are wearing now when he left."

"They always come back when they look like that," Simon agreed.

The two of them shared a laugh, but Caesar scowled as he marched on to the office. He could hope and pray with everything he had for George's return, but what if his sweetheart's conversion truly was just a whim of the moment? What if his father convinced him to see the error of his ways and to view Caesar as the Devil again?

He wasn't certain he could bear it. Playing the Devil in jest was one thing, but when it came to matters of the heart and of his future happiness, Caesar could only pray as he'd never prayed before.

Chapter Nine

An entire day had passed since George had left Perdition, and he felt as though he were in hell. The irony of that feeling was not lost on him. He imagined telling Caesar as much as his father forced him to kneel on the rough cobbles of the alley behind their modest dwelling in a part of London that was supposed to be respectable. Caesar would roar with laughter at the jest, then he would most likely draw George into his arms and whisper rude trifles about how he would make George feel as though he were in Paradise.

Those thoughts had just begun to warm George when yet another bucket of cold water splashed across his head and naked back, jolting him into remembering he was supposed to be praying and doing penance.

"I do not hear the words of Jesus on your lips, boy," his father said in the same sort of voice he used while preaching on street corners. "I do not hear the gospel rising up toward heaven and cleansing you of your sins."

George considered replying. He hadn't said much at all since his father had dragged him away from the first place he had felt loved, the first place he had felt as though his place in the world was clear and his desire to serve others could be fulfilled. There was nothing to say in the face of his father's form of piety.

"I do not hear you," his father barked, moving to stand in front of George, the empty bucket still in his hand. "I do not hear your confession of sin and your show of sincere repentance."

George lifted his gaze from where it had been fixed on the cobbles in front of him to stare at his father. He shivered violently, thanks to the cold water his father had been throwing at him for more than an hour now. It was meant to wash away his sins, or so his father had said, but the gleam in his father's eyes as he surveyed George's wretched state— wet, trembling, naked from the waist up, his trousers soaked, his hair plastered to his head, his lips blue with cold—was far too delighted.

It was a revelation, albeit one that had been creeping up on George for years. His father enjoyed watching him suffer. Not as any sort of sign or token for a vengeful god who demanded obedience, but for his own pleasure. George had never allowed himself to notice before. He hadn't known any different sort of love, only that which his father had professed to have for him.

Now he knew differently. He knew what it felt like to be touched with kindness, with desire. He knew what it was to wake in the arms of a man who smiled at him and treated his body to pleasure beyond knowing. But that was only a fraction of what George had felt with Caesar. He'd been appreciated, cared for. Caesar had given him the ability to truly follow God's command to feed the hungry and tend to the sick. It had been less than two days, but Caesar had given him the chance to be the man he'd always wanted to be. It was as if—

George was smashed out of his thoughts as his father raised a hand and slapped him across the face. George tipped to the side, grinding his already bruised and bloodied knees against the stones.

"The Devil has your mind, I see," his father snarled. He wasn't wrong. "I will beat these sinful thoughts out of you if I must," he continued, walking back to the trough to fill his bucket again.

There was nothing for George to do but straighten, clasp his hands together, and recite, "Yea, though I walk through the valley of the shadow of death," while eyeing his father's back with narrowed eyes.

He had gone back and forth in his mind about whether he should have left Perdition the day before. In the moment, it had felt like the right thing to do, like he was saving Caesar and his partners, and the people who were employed by the club, not to mention the people in Caesar's old neighborhood who depended on him, from his father's misplaced wrath. It had felt like a sacrifice he needed to make to save a hundred souls or more.

Since then, however, a sense of futility had descended on him. His father was like a dog who would not let go of a bone. He had not simply let the matter drop and moved on to further proselytizing and harassing men and women who had better, more useful things to do on the streetcorners of London. Instead, he had put every bit of his energy and dominance into making George's life a living hell.

Another bucket of water splashed into George from the side, stinging his bruised face. He fought to maintain his balance as his father tossed the bucket aside and marched over to George. He grabbed a fistful of George's hair and jerked his head up to look at him.

"Tell me!" his father demanded. "Tell me what sort of sin and depravity you were forced into at the hands of those devils."

George would rather die than whisper a single word of what he and Caesar had shared. It was pure and sacred to him, no matter how his father would see it. Instead of answering, he continued muttering psalms.

"Tell me, you worm!" his father shouted again, shaking George's head. "What were those women who slithered over you and stole your virtue like? How did they seduce you with their nimble bodies and their silken skin? Tell me how they sucked away your soul and forced you to copulate with them. I'd wager you had more than one of them at a time, tempting you into the very grossest of debaucheries."

George's mouth dropped open as he forgot the lines of the beloved psalm. He would have recoiled from his father if he could, particularly since a bulge had appeared in the front of his father's trousers. Could it be that the man was aroused by whatever misadventures he believed George to have had? Did he want a confession of sin or an account of all the pleasures he'd supposedly experienced so that he could revel in them, perhaps even imagine himself in George's place?

"I touched no woman in that way," George snapped.

He had reached the end of his patience with his father and pulled away from the man's grip. His bruised, shivering body was slow to obey his commands, but he stood and glared at his father.

"I was taken in by one of the owners of the club and fed," he said. It wasn't a lie, even if it was not the entire truth. "He treated me with kindness, asked why I felt called to serve God. We went to a poor neighborhood, the place where he was raised, and ministered to the poor there."

"Lies," his father snorted, shaking his head. "You sinned. I can feel it in you."

"I distributed bread to the hungry," George went on, his words gaining more power and his frigid body heating with his zeal. "I comforted the lowly. I even helped to bring a new babe into this world. And I tended to the sick and elderly, sometimes just holding their hands and praying with them when everyone else had forgotten them."

His father sneered as though George had contracted some sort of pox by doing so.

"These are the things Jesus commanded his disciples to do, Father," he insisted, taking a half step toward his father. "This is what any man of God should do, not accosting innocents on street corners and enjoying the sound of his own voice."

"Blasphemy!" his father shouted, reaching out to slap him again. George was able to dodge that blow, but it didn't stop his father from raging on. "The Devil must be scourged out of you. On your knees again, boy. You need more than to be cleansed, you need to be flogged."

His father marched past him, heading back into the house. George watched him go, old fear battling with new incredulity and the knowledge that welled up from his heart that the way Caesar had shown him was the right way.

He hesitated for a moment, staring around him at the soaked cobblestones, the rubbish pile near the kitchen door, and the other kitchen yards for their neighbors' houses that were within his sight. The housekeeper employed by a tailor who lived across the way and several doors down was sweeping her kitchen steps and watching him anxiously. No doubt she had seen the entire

105

confrontation. She smiled sadly at George, then went about her work.

That was all George needed to show him that there was no longer any need for him to stay captive under his father's thumb for a moment longer. He headed toward the house, careless of the cold water dripping from him. There were towels in the kitchen with which he could dry himself before dressing.

He had thought at first that Caesar had captured him and held him prisoner, but the truth was that Caesar had given him the keys to set himself free from the prison his father had locked him in ages ago.

He was on his way from the back of the house to the front, a warm towel wrapped around his sodden trousers and another in his hands as he dried himself when the sound of voices from the front parlor stopped him.

"You say you have proof?" a deep voice George didn't recognize asked.

"Ample proof," his father answered. "The villains kidnapped my son and held him prisoner in the club for two days. He was subjected to every sort of vile torture and depravity."

The unfamiliar man sighed and said, "I mean, you have proof of illegal gambling activity? You've proof that there are card tables, games of chance?"

"That and more," his father said. "Prostitution of the worst sort. There are most likely children being subjected to that wickedness as well."

Fury spilled through George. Perdition did not employ children. He had not seen a single soul who was not of adult age within the building the entire time he'd been there. And while it was possible they could be elsewhere in the house, he refused to believe Caesar or his partners would condone such activity.

"I will require testimony in order to send runners in to put a stop to the activities of the hell," the unfamiliar voice went on. "Though we are aware of the nature of the establishment, we cannot take action unless several reliable witnesses testify against it."

"I will provide all the testimony you need," George's father said. "My son will speak against the place as well. He will tell you of the wickedness he was forced to suffer."

George's eyes went wide and his pulse raced. He tiptoed along the hall, heading for the stairs and up to his bedchamber as silently as he could. His father would have to employ much more than buckets of cold water or physical abuse to convince him to say a single word against Perdition. The frightening thing was that he knew his father would try all those things and more to get his own way.

George peeled out of his wet trousers, dried himself as best he could, and dressed quickly in his own, simple clothing. His father had forced him to strip out of the finer things he'd borrowed from Caesar the day before and had burned them while George watched. Those few articles of clothing had been expensive. If his father truly cared for the things he professed to care about, he could have sold them and given the money to those in need. Instead, he'd chosen to destroy that of which he did not approve.

As soon as he was dressed, George packed up the very few items of his own that he did not wish to leave behind and took that achingly small sack with him when he headed back downstairs. The parlor was silent, suggesting that his father's guest had not stayed. It was probably safer for all that way.

George headed straight for the door and reached for the

handle, but hesitated. He could walk out without a word, possibly never to see his father again, but something about that made him feel as though he were leaving with his tail tucked between his legs. His father would make up some story of his cowardly, sinful nature, and likely go about the rest of his life believing himself to be the better man. It was not something George should care about, but the tiny shoot of pride that years of his father's abuse had left him with questioned whether that was the best way to go.

The decision of how to leave was made for him when his father's shout of, "What are you doing, boy, and where do you think you're going?" boomed from the other end of the hall.

George turned to see his father coming out of the kitchen, looking furious.

"I have not given you leave to end your penance," his father continued as he marched up to George. "You should be on your knees, abject and miserable with your sins, begging for mercy from me and from God."

George's heart lurched in his chest. Perhaps he was hearing it for the first time, or perhaps he had heard it all along and ignored it, but it was suddenly clear to him that his father believed himself to be God's spokesman. Perhaps he believed himself to be God himself.

"I am leaving, Father," he said with surprising calm. The decision was made, and he knew it was the right one. There was no need for him to tarry or to question his choices anymore.

His father's eyes went wide. "You have no right to leave me, boy."

George drew in a slow breath. "Yes, I do," he said. "I am a man in my own right, and I have seen the truth of things at last."

"The truth of things," his father said with a scornful snort. He opened his mouth to say more, but George cut him off.

"I have lived under your roof and under your thumb for too long," he said, taking a step toward his father and towering over him, even though they were of a similar height. "You claim to want to do God's work, but I have not once seen you serve the poor. I have never seen you comfort the dying or visit widows and orphans. You have done nothing to make the lives of those around you better."

"I have spoken God's word," his father protested, though for the first time, George could see worry in his eyes —not over the possibility he had done wrong, but rather fear that George might treat him with the same violence he had always shown to his only child.

"You have listened to the sound of your own voice," George told him. "You have not listened to the cries of help, cries that have arisen from God's own creations. I want no part of your theology anymore, Father," he went on when his father looked like he wanted to get a word in. "I have been shown another way—one of love and light. I wish to help people, not harangue them with so-called truth. I wish to love my fellow men and to be loved by them."

It was the closest he could come to sharing his feelings for Caesar, but those sentiments were, perhaps, the fuel that fed the fire in his heart—not just to commence with a love affair with the dashing, wicked, beautiful, kind man, but to work with him to ease the suffering of others.

"I am leaving," George finished, reaching for the doorhandle again. "Do not expect to ever see me again. I am quite certain that from henceforth, we will live our lives in different circles entirely. I will be happy there, which is all you need to know. And I hope you will find some modicum of happiness in this path you have chosen for yourself. Goodbye."

George pulled open the door and stepped out into the warm morning sunshine. He felt like a man who had released the shackles that had held him for most of his life and who was stepping into freedom.

But before he had taken more than a handful of steps, his father raced out onto the doorstep and shouted, "You will regret this! Before the day is done, you will be rotting in gaol along with your demon accomplices. The law is about to descend on that gaming hell, and if you are there, it will rain down on you as well, mark my words."

George didn't stop walking and didn't turn back to acknowledge his father's words, but they filled him with a sense of dread all the same. The man with whom he had been speaking earlier could only be a Bow Street runner. His father had likely arranged for some sort of raid on Perdition, and by the sound of things, it would happen before the day was done.

George picked up his pace, hoping he could reach Caesar before it was too late. There had to be something they could do to prevent disaster, some way to ensure Perdition's continued safety. He might not have the power to stop his father on his own, but if he and Caesar, and the other partners, could combine forces, he was certain they could fend off any evil.

Chapter Ten

The anonymous tip that Perdition was soon to be under attack reached Caesar's, Jasper's, and Simon's ears before dawn. Caesar had been the first to receive word that the Bow Street runners had their eyes on the club and that some sort of invasion would take place that day, not because he held the most authority at the club, but because he had been up before dawn, pacing the hallways in an attempt to fight the restlessness that hadn't left him since George had left the morning before.

Caesar hadn't been able to sit still for more than a few minutes since the moment his beautiful curate had been dragged away by his father. George hadn't been dragged bodily. He had left on his own power, but Caesar could not shake the feeling that Rev. Mulgrew had forced George to take a course of action he never would have otherwise.

He hadn't been able to sleep that night and had waited near one of the windows in the front parlor. Jasper had laughed at him for peering out into the street like a lovesick debutante every five minutes to see if George had somehow returned to his former pulpit. Simon had lost his humor about the situation when Caesar refused to eat or drink anything, despite Cook preparing all his favorite foods for supper. Things had gotten so bad that Giles even offered to suck his cock to help Caesar fall asleep when he was still pacing the floors after midnight.

Receiving word that they were in danger of a raid was a welcome relief, when all was said and done. It had been just the thing Caesar needed to spur him into actions that might bear some fruit. As dawn broke across St. James's, he'd gone upstairs, washed, shaved, and dressed, then come back downstairs to issue every sort of order to conceal Perdition's less than legal activities and to make the club look as though it were little more than a teahouse where men sometimes also engaged in whist.

It was swiftly approaching noon, all of the whores employed by the club had been dressed in exceedingly modest clothing, Caesar and Simon were in the process of hiding the ledgers containing records of some of the high and mighty's most outrageous gambling debts, and Jasper was overseeing an extremely high stakes game of Commerce that had been moved to the servants' dining room downstairs so that it might evade interruption, if the runners did arrive, when a knock sounded on the front door. Caesar didn't give it much thought. Perdition was a hive of activity, with gentlemen of means paying calls at any time of day.

But when his sweetheart's cry of, "Caesar," sounded from the hallway behind him as he locked the cupboard in the office that now contained the ledgers, Caesar whipped around to face the doorway so fast that he nearly lost his balance.

George was there, right there, rushing into the office. Caesar's heart thrilled with affection and relief for one beautiful moment before he noticed how much the worse for wear his darling looked. George was dressed in ragged clothing—even worse than what he'd come to Perdition wearing three days before—his hair was damp and matted, his skin was pale, but worst of all, an ugly, splotchy bruise covered one side of his face.

Caesar guessed in a moment that George's father had somehow caused that bruise. His feelings of relief changed instantly to rage as he dropped the cupboard key on the desk and flew to his beloved.

"My God, what did he do to you?" he demanded. He nearly embraced George, but instead he placed his hands gently on the man's face and turned it so that he could get a better view of the bruise.

"It matters not," George said, shaking his head and dislodging Caesar's hands as he did. He then did what Caesar had intended from the start and threw his arms around Caesar, hugging him tight. "Nothing matters, now that I'm here, with you."

The relief in George's voice was second only to the way his body sagged against Caesar's. Caesar set aside his fury long enough to embrace George in return and to kiss him. What he'd intended to be a short kiss of welcome turned into a passionate meeting of mouths. As soon as George parted his lips for him, he wanted—nay, needed—everything he could get from George. He thrust his tongue into his beloved's mouth then moaned when George flipped the balance of power between them to invade his mouth.

It was glorious and wonderful, and Caesar could have drowned in their kiss, but movement out of the corner of his eyes caused him to pull away. Jasper had been taken as much by surprise as Caesar by George's entrance, and, with a grin on his face, he slipped discreetly from the room to give the two of them a modicum of privacy.

Before Jasper could leave entirely, George called out, "Wait!" He pivoted to face Jasper, his arms still wrapped around Caesar. "Do not go yet. I've come with news of great importance."

"The only important news I want to know is where your father is so that I can wring his neck for striking you, as he has clearly done," Caesar said, his voice a ferocious growl. He brushed his fingertips over George's bruised face.

George sent him a look of remorse and love that nearly melted Caesar's heart before saying, "My father has done worse than that." He glanced between Caesar and Jasper, then said, "He has contacted the Bow Street runners and given an account of what he believes takes place here. For whatever reason, the runner who was at his house this morning believes him, and I am reasonably certain there will be a raid on Perdition before the day is done."

"Is that why you have come here?" Caesar asked, his heart beating hard in his chest. "To warn us? Is that all?"

George pivoted back to him, letting out a breath that seemed to contain a wealth of worries and cares that he was letting go of as well. "No," he said, cradling Caesar's face in one hand. "That is the least of the reasons I returned. I am here because I could not stay away. You may think me as foolish as you'd like, but two days was all it took for me to recognize my heart's true home."

Caesar caught his breath. He wasn't certain he enjoyed feeling like a green lad with his first *tendre*, but George's words made his insides flutter. "Truly?" he asked with an expression of hope.

"Truly," George repeated with a smile. "I only left yesterday because I thought I was helping you, saving you, by deflecting my father's attention. But the moment he grabbed me by the ear once we were in the street—as

114

though I were still a small child and not the man I know I am—I knew it was a grievous error on my part. I allowed him to take me home and to rail at me and put me through what he saw as penance for my sins, but I see no sin, I see no wrong at all."

"He has injured you," Caesar said, scowling and touching George's bruises again. "Perhaps more than I can see at this moment."

George flushed, but instead of confirming Caesar's guess—though his look was confirmation enough—he said, "The moment I realized there was no changing my father's mind or distracting him from what he sees as holy vengeance, I abandoned him and that way of life. I want to be with you," he went on, closing both hands around Caesar's face and leaning in to gently kiss his lips. "I only ever want to be with you, from now until the end of my days. I have nothing at all to bring with me. I fear I shall be quite dependent on you at first, but I will work for my keep. I will do whatever you need of me in order to earn my place here with you, in Perdition."

The clever smile he added to the end of his beautiful words would have melted Caesar's heart, if it hadn't already been melted.

"Yes, darling, of course," Caesar replied. He leaned toward George, kissing him with all the passion that his beloved had shown him. "Yes, a thousand times over. I do not need you to work to earn your keep either. I want you here the way I want the finest foods in my belly and the softest silks against my skin. I want you inside me and around me as well," he said, adding a saucy wink.

George laughed and moved in for another kiss, but he stopped at the last moment and drew in an alarmed breath. "My father and the Bow Street runners are on their way, I am certain," he said, turning to address Jasper as well.

"We already know," Jasper said with a grin that was entirely too charmed and satisfied for the danger they found themselves in. "We were alerted to as much by an anonymous source this morning."

"Then...then you do not need me here?" George asked, looking the slightest bit disappointed.

"Of course, we need you here, love," Caesar said, kissing him quickly, then stepping back to grasp George's hand. "We need you here desperately."

Caesar led him from the office. Jasper followed.

"We've relocated the card games already in progress," Jasper said, "and everything else that can be covered over or swept under the carpet has been taken care of. All we can do now is—"

There was no need for his answer and no need for waiting. Caesar, George, and Jasper made it only halfway up the hall before one of the lads opened the door and let Rev. Mulgrew and what appeared to be four, burly runners into Perdition.

"Do you see?" Rev. Mulgrew demanded immediately, throwing out his arm to point at George with a scowl. "Do you see what kind of villainy this hell is guilty of?"

An awkward silence followed his questions.

Caesar knew the game they were playing, and he did his best to appear both dignified and perplexed. "I beg your pardon?" he asked.

"Gentlemen, is there something I could assist you with?" Jasper asked as though Rev. Mulgrew and the runners were ordinary callers instead of invaders with ill-intent.

The runners fell into cautious but alert looks. Rev.

Mulgrew seemed enraged that he had not walked into an orgy.

"Tear this place down brick by brick if you must," he snarled. "Dens of sin of this sort must be eradicated at all cost."

One of the runners—a thick-set man with arms as wide as tree trunks and grey streaks in his dark hair stepped forward. "We were given information that one of London's most notorious gaming hells operates out of this house," he said.

George gasped at Caesar's side and leaned close to him. "I know that voice," he whispered. "He is the man who came to my father's house this morning."

Caesar nodded, but the conversation had already moved on.

"This is no gaming hell," Jasper laughed. He approached the runner with an easy manner and held out his hand. "Allow me to introduce myself. I am Jasper Black. And you are?"

"Theophilus Brunner," the runner introduced himself, taking Jasper's hand awkwardly. "The information I have gathered about this place is sound. I demand to be allowed to search the premises."

Caesar caught his breath. It was exactly what they expected to have demanded of them, and they had done their best to conceal anything that might be considered incriminating. But there was no telling how thorough the runners would be in their search. Certain objects—such as the questionable artwork that adorned the place—could not be so easily hidden or explained away, however.

"Of course," Jasper said with a gracious bow. He stepped to the side and gestured toward the hallway, as though nothing gave him more pleasure than allowing

Brunner the full run of the house. "Be my guest. Would you care for tea? Giles, bring our guests tea."

Caesar hadn't noticed Giles watching the unfolding scene from the top of the stairs. He held his breath for a moment, praying that Giles had put on clothing for a change—the young man had made it clear from the start that he much preferred to exist in the state Nature had made him.

"Yes, sir," Giles answered, rushing down the stairs—dressed as modestly as any university scholar—and skidding to a halt in front of Brunner. His eyes went wide as he gazed up at the beefy man, and he broke out in a hazy, lopsided grin. "Hello," he greeted Brunner, as though he were a favored client.

Brunner narrowed his eyes and growled at Giles—which only made the lad whimper and sway a bit.

Unfortunately, his reaction did not go unnoticed.

"Do you see?" Rev. Mulgrew demanded, gesturing to Giles with wide eyes, his mouth agape. "This lad is quite clearly a whore, and a whore of the very worst, most illegal sort at that."

"He is no such thing," Jasper said, looking and sounding thoroughly scandalized. "How dare you?"

Simon chose that moment to emerge from the back of the hall. "What is going on here?" he asked.

"Giles was just about to fetch tea for our guests," Caesar said, stepping forward to join the scene at last. George moved cautiously with him. "Weren't you, Giles?"

"Yes, sir." Giles dragged his gaze away from Brunner and dashed down the hall, face pink, eyes filled with stars.

Caesar shook his head at the lad as he left. It was a good thing they'd sent him away. The lad knew what he liked, and that was men like Brunner. Keeping the two in the same room would unravel their deceit within seconds.

"What guests are these?" Simon asked, coming to stand in the hall beside Caesar and eyeing the runners suspiciously.

"They're Bow Street runners," Caesar said, as though he'd never heard anything so ridiculous. "They seem to think we're operating a gaming hell here." He laughed loudly as if to say the idea were absurd.

"Why are you simply standing there?" Rev. Mulgrew demanded. "Why have you not torn this place down and taken these devils off to gaol. Are you lot that useless?"

Caesar fought to hide his smile as Brunner turned to gape incredulously at the man. Rev. Mulgrew was making no friends with his manic behavior.

"I will ask the questions," Brunner said. He crossed his arms and stared at Jasper, Caesar, and Simon in succession. "What is this house, if not a gaming hell? Do you all reside here, and if so, for what purpose? What is the meaning of such lascivious artwork?" He nodded to a painting of nymphs and satyrs. Caesar knew the artwork would give them away. Brunner swallowed and flushed slightly, then asked, "Who was that strange young man, Giles?"

Caesar's brow inched up. So Brunner was interested in Giles? Perhaps they could gain a customer rather than losing their entire enterprise.

The trouble was, there was no good answer to Brunner's sharp questions. Caesar and the others had had time to hide incriminating evidence, but they had not come up with an alternative story.

Once again, it was as though fate intervened on their behalf. Or, if not fate, then the success of the missive he'd sent off with the hall boy in the early hours of the morning, immediately after they'd learned of the threat facing them.

"This house is mine," a strong, authoritative voice declared.

Everyone turned to the far end of the hall. Giles held the door to downstairs open, and none other than Caesar's father stepped into the hall and strode up to join them, dripping power and authority. Caesar beamed with pride, even more so when his father winked at him.

"Your Grace," Brunner said, dropping immediately into a bow. "I...I did not expect to see you here. I didn't know this house belonged to you."

"It most certainly does," Caesar's father said. He glanced down his nose at the runners, then curled his lip in derision at Rev. Mulgrew. "I own this house. It is, at present, being used as a reformatory for young people of questionable character." He glanced to Caesar, eyes sparkling with mirth as he spoke.

Caesar half rolled his eyes at his father's teasing. He wished he'd had the chance to speak to the man beforehand to sort out a likelier tale. Proclaiming the house to be a reformatory would not exactly lift them above suspicion.

Brunner shuffled awkwardly, his expression hinting that he was caught between contradicting the word of a duke and doing his duty. "I was given information that one of London's most notorious gaming hells operates from here," he said, sending Rev. Mulgrew a vicious look.

Caesar's father barked a laugh. "Did you hear that?" he asked Caesar, then glanced to Jasper and Simon. "A gaming hell! Imagine that."

They all laughed as though the notion were ridiculous. None of them denied it, though.

Caesar's father cleared his throat. "You gentlemen have

been misinformed. This house belongs to me and is under my protection." He sent Brunner a particularly pointed look. "I suggest you leave and direct your inquiries to other houses of vice that litter this city. You need not concern yourself with this place."

It was an order as surely as anything. Rev. Mulgrew looked as though he might actually argue with a duke. Whatever force held him back, he quivered with rage and turned a vivid shade of puce with the effort it took him to stay silent.

"It appears the information I was given was incorrect," Brunner grumbled, shooting another furious look at Rev. Mulgrew. "My apologies for intruding, Your Grace."

"We will say no more of it," Caesar's father said. "Ever again," he added with terrifying finality.

Brunner didn't say another word, but Caesar could tell he wanted to. Even though he turned to leave, ushering Rev. Mulgrew out with him, Caesar had the distinct feeling that was not the last they would see of Brunner.

Rev. Mulgrew turned just as he reached the door and glared at George. "You are no longer any son of mine. You are lost to me and to all righteous people forever. May you burn in hell."

With that, he stepped through the door, slamming it behind him.

"What an irritating little bug of a man," Caesar's father commented, flicking an imaginary bit of fluff off the end of his sleeve and sniffing.

Caesar laughed out loud. "Father, you are the very best *deus ex machina* and the very best of men that I have ever known," he said, striding to his father and embracing the man. His father laughed and embraced him in return, but the gesture only lasted a moment before Caesar pulled back and said, "No, that is no longer correct." He moved to George's side, taking his sweetheart's hand and bringing him forward. "This is the best man I have ever met."

Caesar's father glanced down his nose at George and asked, "And you are?"

Caesar knew his father well enough to know he was intimidating George on purpose. And it worked.

"G-george Mulgrew," George answered, barely able to get out his own name.

Caesar clasped George's arm, hugging it close. "George is my paramour, Father, and the kindest, most generous, most blessed man you will ever meet."

"Is he now?" Caesar's father raised his eyebrows and looked to Jasper and Simon as if for confirmation.

"Mulgrew is a good man," Simon said with a shrug. "Your son loves him."

"And that is the finest recommendation that could be given," Caesar's father said with a smile. He glanced down the hall to where Giles had reemerged with a large tray set with tea things. "Ah! Perfect timing. Shall we all adjourn to one of these lovely parlors for tea so that I might learn more about today's goings on? And about my son's new favorite, of course."

Caesar's father headed straight into the parlor to the left, gesturing for Giles to bring the tea as though he truly did own the house, which he did not. Caesar smiled from ear to ear. He loved his father, and it was a rare treat to spend time with him. Even more so to be able to introduce George.

George sent Caesar an astounded look as he followed into the parlor. "Your father is the Duke of—"

Caesar raised a finger to his lips to stop him. "It is a secret," he whispered.

George grinned, reaching for Caesar's hand. "I do not know whom to be more in awe of," he said. "Him or you."

"Oh, me," Caesar said. "Most definitely me."

The rest of the day was spent in absolute bliss, as far as Caesar was concerned. His father could only stay for an hour, but they had a jolly time sharing tea and swapping stories of both Caesar's and his father's latest exploits. His father asked insightful questions about George and about his plans, now that he had broken with his father. It was revealed to George that Caesar's father financed most of Caesar's charitable endeavors, and when Caesar's father learned of George's calling and his desire to serve the poor, the gears were set in motion for George to be given some sort of position of employment in his father's charitable endeavors.

After the duke departed, Caesar and George helped Jasper and Simon to set Perdition back in order. It seemed to take longer to set the place up again than it had to rush everything into hiding to begin with.

"I doubt we will be safe from Bow Street indefinitely," Simon said as they returned chairs to the card tables in one of the back parlors. "Dogs like that do not give up until they have their bone."

"Will you be safe, though?" George asked, genuine concern in his eyes.

"Will *we* be safe you mean," Caesar told him with a wink. "For you are one of us now, my darling."

George blushed, and since no one was around but the two of them, Jasper and Simon, he caught Caesar's hand and pulled him in for a kiss.

"Yes," he said, then stole a second kiss. "Will *we* be safe?"

"We will," Caesar promised. "As long as you and I are

together, we shall always be safe. We will keep each other from any harm."

Caesar grinned and leaned toward George's lips, but Jasper snorted and said, "Sentimental treacle. The two of you are preposterous."

"Agreed," Simon said. "Get yourselves and your silliness out of here. Go upstairs and work it off until you can be around sensible people again."

George opened his mouth as if to say something apologetic, but Caesar grabbed his hand and tugged him toward the door. "We do not mind if we do," he said, rushing George out of the room.

They burst into laughter, like two boys Giles's age, and hurried down the hall to the stairs, already unbuttoning their jackets.

By the time they made it up to Caesar's bedchamber, they'd loosened their clothes, and once they crossed the room to Caesar's bed, most of their clothing had already been shed. They tumbled into bed together in a mass of arms and legs, heated skin, sighs and moans, and grasping hands.

"I was worried you would not return," Caesar panted as he struggled to remove his boots and peel back the bedcovers at the same time.

"What?" George paused in the middle of throwing his shoes aside and gaped at Caesar. "You doubted for so much as a moment whether I would come back to you? After all we shared?"

Caesar shoved aside his other boot and his breeches with it, leaving him naked. "No, not truly," he said, grinning and splaying himself for George's perusal. "My heart knew what my head doubted for a moment."

George tutted as he kicked off his own breeches, then

crawled between Caesar's open legs. "I am not certain I can accept that answer," he said, planting his hands on the bed on either side of Caesar's shoulders and staring down at him with a mock frown. "Surely you must know my place in this life, and perhaps the next, is here with you."

Caesar purred at the sweetness of that sentiment, then reached up to grasp the back of George's neck. He pulled him down roughly for a kiss, reveling in the fact that he could take the receiving role and still utterly control the way the two of them were together.

"I may never let you out of my sight again, you realize," he panted as he stroked his hands over George's body, pinching his nipples briefly. "You do tend to wander off and get yourself into trouble when you are left unchaperoned."

George chuckled, then let out a sigh. "In spite of spending the first part of my life under my father's thumb, I do not think I would mind spending the rest of it under yours."

Caesar grew as serious as George was for a moment. He swept his fingertips over the ugly bruise on George's face. "I regret that I did not have time to thrash your father soundly before he left here. I could murder the man for what he's done to you."

George shrugged without meeting Caesar's eyes, then dipped down to lay a series of kisses across the top of his chest. "Bruises will fade, and soon enough, I am certain the memory of that man's cruelty will as well. I have much to look forward to that will replace the false lessons my father tried to teach me."

"I will give you a true education, my love," Caesar said, threading his fingers through George's hair as his sweetheart dusted his chest with more kisses. He made an approving sound, then said, "Beginning with instruction on how best to please me."

"Oh?" George glanced up at him with a grin.

"Yes, it begins with you inching down a bit more and opening your mouth to receive a certain part of me," he said.

George laughed and blushed, then did just as Caesar said and slithered lower. "Like this?" He grasped the base of Caesar's cock, stroking it a few times before lowering himself to kiss the tip, then to lavish Caesar's head with licks and sucks that had Caesar gripping handfuls of the bedclothes.

For a novice, George certainly showed talent. He was particularly generous with his tongue, and he seemed to enjoy driving Caesar mad by sucking powerfully on just his tip. He attempted to take more and more of him with a series of short bobbing movements, but that only lasted until he ended up gagging himself by being too ambitious. After that, he was more hesitant.

"Never mind, love," Caesar panted. "You've driven me quite mad enough. I want you thrusting in me now."

George's eyes lit with a smoldering excitement, particularly when Caesar reached to the side table and retrieved the jar there.

"I cannot decide if this method of congress is as wicked as my father has always said every sort of libidinous behavior is or if it is God's cleverest creation," George panted as he slicked his cock.

"Can it not be both?" Caesar asked. He then unceremoniously pulled his legs back and arched his hips up to rest his ankles on George's shoulders, winking as he did.

George sputtered with laughter, but managed to move himself into a satisfactory position and push all the same. "Utterly diabolical," he groaned, his words fading into a pleasured cry as he pushed past Caesar's body's momentary resistance and settled in deep.

Caesar groaned and pushed against George to drive him deeper. "If God did not wish men to love and enjoy each other, He would not have designed us to bring each other bliss," he sighed. "Now fuck me harder. Truly make me feel it."

"Yes, sir," George said on a gasp, in imitation of Perdition's servants.

George may have been a novice, but he was an enthusiastic one. He found his rhythm, catching just the right spot within Caesar as he did so, and pounded into him with abandon. Caesar reached for one of George's hands as it gripped his thigh and held it in a gesture of intimacy that went beyond the physical connection they'd created. He grasped his cock with the other to provide just enough friction to send him soaring as George lost himself in their union.

All too soon, they were both teetering over the edge, and when George's face contorted as his control snapped and he spilled himself inside of Caesar, Caesar couldn't help but respond by joining him in orgasmic bliss. His release felt all the more beautiful, knowing that he and George were at the beginning of their journey together instead of simply stealing a moment that would pass and be gone.

"I love you," George gasped as all energy seemed to leave him. He pulled out, then collapsed atop Caesar with a groan. "I know it is sudden and mad, but I do, I love you."

Caesar wrapped himself around George and rolled him until they lay side by side, entangled with each other. "I love you as well, my darling savior. And I will forevermore."

* * *

I hope you've enjoyed Caesar and George's story! There's so much more to come from *The Perdition Club*! Next up is *Black & White*, by Ruby Moone! Keep clicking to get started on Chapter One....

If you enjoyed this book and would like to hear more from me, please sign up for my newsletter! When you sign up, you'll get a free, full-length MM Regency novella, *Rendezvous in Paris*. It's part of my *Tales from the Grand Tour* series, but can be read as a stand-alone. Pick up your free copy today by signing up to receive my newsletter (which I only send out when I have a new release)!

Sign up here: http://eepurl.com/cbaVMH

Are you on social media? I am! Come and join the fun on Facebook: http://www.facebook.com/merryfarmerreaders

I'm also a huge fan of Instagram and post lots of original content there: https://www.instagram.com/merryfarmer/

And now, it's time to get started on *Black & White*, by Ruby Moone!

Chapter One

Alexander White edged his way around Perdition with no small amount of caution. Not *literally*, he thought with a smile borne more of a very fine claret than wit. He'd watched the staff from the exceedingly fine gaming hell coming and going and identified the doors they used. With an eye on the two gentlemen he had just relieved of a considerable sum, he'd slipped through one of the staff doors unnoticed. Or so he hoped. It was clear to Alex that Laurence Hartigan had lost with good grace. However, he feared Miles Cross may decide to retrieve his vowels in a less than gentlemanly fashion. Even in his inebriated state, Alex realised it would be sensible to put himself out of harm's way.

He leaned his head against the closed door for a moment, trying to get a grip on himself. Damn Freddy Mackenzie and his drinking games. He was utterly cast away. He took several deep breaths and tried to make his eyes focus and the room stop spinning, to no avail. Not at all. He sniggered at the realisation.

Pausing to steady himself, he set off down the corridor. His gait wobbled and his shoulder bounced off the elegantly panelled wall, so he paused for a moment, gathering his balance and his composure. He grinned. He should cast himself to Perdition more often! He laughed quietly at his own cleverness. With an exaggerated effort he stood upright, pointed himself in what he guessed was the right direction, and headed down the richly carpeted corridor. He hoped he could find a way out, or even somewhere to hide until it was safe to leave.

There were portraits hanging at regular intervals, interspersed with candles in sconces. Alex tried to focus on them as he walked, but they danced about. He sucked in a breath, steadied himself, and when he was sure he could walk without mishap, continued. If only the lights in the sconces along the corridor would stop moving *quite* so much, he'd feel right as a trivet.

He bounced off the wall again, but sallied forth and

rounded the corner, only to run into an immovable object. He let out a yell, flailed, and fell flat on his arse with enough of a thump to rattle his teeth.

"Christ!" he wheezed from his prone position before looking up. On doing so, he stared. And stared. Looming over him was a man. Tall, broad of shoulder, firm chin, dark curling hair, and startling blue eyes a man could lose himself in for days on end.

He flopped back, propped up only by his elbows, let his legs spread, and grinned. "Well, hello Goliath." He chuckled at his witticism.

Goliath frowned. A deep, dark scowl suggesting his brows might be permanently fixed in that position. Alex's grin widened. A grumpy Goliath!

"Who the hell are you?"

Alex licked his lips and tried not to squint as the man seemed to waver. He gave him his best seductive smile and pitched his voice low.

"Alexander White, at your service." He allowed his upraised knees to part even more invitingly. He wanted to giggle but kept a straight face. Goliath's lips parted as he looked over Alex's prone form, and even in his inebriated state, he heard the hitch in his breathing. Any thought of humour fled at that soft, breathy sound. Alexander's mouth was instantly dry, heart thumping hard against his ribs, and his cock valiantly tried to rise in his breeches. He licked his lips and attempted to speak, but no words would come.

Goliath sighed and shook his head, breaking the spell. "Drunk as a fucking wheelbarrow," he muttered. Alexander nodded, forced to agree with his estimation.

The man reached down and held out a hand. Alexander took it and allowed himself to be hauled to his feet. He wobbled dangerously, and Goliath grabbed his arms to steady him.

"Thank you," Alexander whispered, nose suddenly very close to a cleanly-shaven cheek that smelled of sandalwood and warm man. He breathed in and let his eyes flutter closed as he leaned against him.

"Stop that," Goliath muttered, but made no attempt to move him away. Alex took this as a signal, as any red-blooded male might, that his attentions were welcome, and nuzzled his nose against Goliath's cheek.

"Mmmm," he murmured and moved sinuously closer. He leaned against the man, largely because he was finding it increasingly difficult to stand unaided, but also because he was terribly drawn by his size and strength. His grumpy Goliath wasn't an awful lot taller than him, but would make two or three of him in bulk. He kissed Goliath's cheek and sighed happily.

Goliath shifted his stance to take Alex's weight. "Are you here with someone?"

"I am indeed. They seem to have disappeared, as have the gaming tables." He looked about and shrugged. "Most irritating and, one must say, inconvenient." At least he had enough wit left to lie.

"How did you get back here?"

"The privvy."

Goliath snorted. "The privvy is nowhere near here."

Alexander managed a sage nod. "I know. I've been walking for damned hours." He snuggled closer and tried to wrap his arms about Goliath's waist, only to find himself rudely repulsed.

"Oh no you don't. We need to get you back to your party and somewhere safe."

"But I like it here with you."

Alex's eyes were closing. He was losing the battle, he could feel it. "Do you like it here with me?" He turned his head and pressed a soft kiss against Goliath's cheek again, breathing in that warm smell of handsome man. "Might you like to kiss me? Hmm?"

"How in God's name have you *lived* this long if this is how you go about things?"

"Hmm?" Alexander tried to press his hips against the bulk that held him at a distance. "S'okay if you don' like kissing." God, were his words slurring? His mouth felt disconnected from the rest of him. Most upsetting, particularly as he was dressed for an interesting evening. He decided he should, in all fairness, make his companion aware of this.

He batted his eyelashes and tried again to speak. "You should know that I," he managed with some gravity, "am wearing my most alluring undergarments." He nodded at Goliath in confirmation and waited for a reaction. Usually by now he was being kissed and shoved against the wall but there appeared to be no response.

He cleared his throat and attempted to clarify. He tried for a seductive wink.

"Silk," he whispered. "Silk and lace." He followed this with another sage nod and a wave of his hand in front of his nether regions.

And that was all Alexander White offered before he crumpled inelegantly against his rescuer, and quietly passed out.

If you're ready to read more, you can get *Black & White here...*

About the Author

I hope you have enjoyed *The Sinner's Gamble*. If you'd like to be the first to learn about when new books in the series come out and more, please sign up for my newsletter here: http://eepurl.com/cbaVMH And remember, Read it, Review it, Share it! For a complete list of works by Merry Farmer with links, please visit http://wp.me/P5ttjb-14F.

Merry Farmer is an award-winning novelist who lives in suburban Philadelphia with her cats, Justine and Peter. She has been writing since she was ten years old and realized one day that she didn't have to wait for the teacher to assign a creative writing project to write something. It was the best day of her life. She then went on to earn not one but two degrees in History so that she would always have something to write about. Her books have reached the Top 100 at Amazon, iBooks, and Barnes & Noble, and have been named finalists in the prestigious RONE and Rom Com Reader's Crown awards.

Acknowledgments

I owe a huge debt of gratitude to my awesome beta-readers, Caroline Lee and Jolene Stewart, for their suggestions and advice. And double thanks to Julie Tague, for being a truly excellent editor and to Cindy Jackson for being an awesome assistant!

Click here for a complete list of other works by Merry Farmer.

Made in the USA
Middletown, DE
27 September 2022